About the Author

Mrs. Diane Martin was born in Chicago, Illinois and currently lives in the Chicago-land area. She earned her Master of Arts and Bachelor of Arts degree from Chicago State University.

My writing legacy would be my true depiction of life; exploring the entire colorful spectrum of people, both good and bad, capturing it in words and exposing it to all cultures in a respectful manner - In a way that would stand the test of time.
- Diane Martin

First Edition

Edited by Dr. William A. Martin & Diane Martin

Interior Design by Diane Martin

Cover Design by Denise Billups of Borel Graphics

Printed by Createspace

Printed in the United States

ISBN 10: 0-9975761-1-1

ISBN 13: 978-0-9975761-1-5

Disclaimer: This is a book of fiction and not based on actual events. Any similarities to current events, characters, names and locations are purely coincidental and based solely on the imagination of the author.

Enjoy Martin

[signature]

Officer
Friendly

Diane Martin

http://dianemartin.weebly.com

"Until lions have their own historians, tales of the hunt shall always glorify the hunter."

- African Proverb

Prologue~

Chicago 2015

"Don't hurt me," I begged. He and his boys pointed and laughed at me. "Please…I'll give you anything you want…just don't hurt me." The young man who was pulling at my blouse, laughed as he said, "There is no doubt in my mind…you are going to give me what I want and then you are going to give my boys what they want too." They all began to laugh. I looked around to see where I was – hoping that someone would walk by, but no one did. The streets were cold, dark, and silent. There was no one, but me and them.

The two other young men laughed. I surveyed my surroundings again. We were in an alley – somewhere off of a busy street.

I looked up at the apartments and found an old lady looking out of her window. Through tears in my eyes, I stared at her. I didn't want to scream for fear of making my attackers angry. I looked at her, pleadingly, through gritted teeth, I mouthed, "Help me." She looked at me. I looked at her. She shook her head and then closed her curtains.

"Noooooooo," I mumbled, under my breath. "No, please no…"

"No, what?" the young man said, as he pressed against me.

"No, please don't do this," I said.

They all began to laugh again. I began to cry. Then the one who seemed to be the leader said, "Save your tears…I promise…this is going to feel really good."

Each one of them began to unbuckle their pants. I pleaded with them again. The leader raised his hand and as his knuckles met the side of my face, he said, "Shut the fuck up and take this shit like a woman."

I closed my eyes. My face felt hot where he'd hit me – so hot that the tears that rolled down my face quickly evaporated. My breathing was so heavy that I could not hear my heart pounding against my chest. He pulled my hand

and placed it on his crotch. "That's it, baby. Grab it. Show BIG daddy how much you want it."

"Come on man…save some for me," one of the young men said, as he touched himself. The other young man watched quietly – waiting patiently for his turn.

Suddenly, I heard the heel of a shoe as it hit the pavement. We all looked in the direction of the sound. A woman walked passed, but something made her turn and come back.

"What are you doing? Let her go!" she shouted, pulling out her cellphone.

The leader turned to her and said, "Hey, why don't you come and join us? You can keep my boys busy while I take care of this. Then when I'm done, I can throw you a little 'taste'. Not sure how much I will have left, but I'll see what I can do." They all laughed.

The woman looked at them and said, "I'm calling the police."

The leader laughed and said, "I don't give a fuck if you call yo' mama. Matter of fact, call yo' mama and let's get this party started."

His boys said, "Yeah...," and slapped each other's hands.

She frowned and then looked at me before running down the sidewalk.

I screamed out to her. "Please....noooo...come back!!!"

"Shut the fuck up." He forced me to my knees. He held my face and said, "If you bite me bitch, I'm going to fucking kill you. Do you understand?"

I nodded my head, "Yes."

He pulled down his pants and pulled my face towards his zipper. "Open wide," he instructed.

I closed my eyes and slowly opened my mouth. Suddenly, I heard a popping sound and then something whirled passed my head. I heard something hit the ground. When I opened my eyes, I saw one of the boys lying on the ground holding his chest. Then, I heard the popping sound again. I turned to my right and another body fell to the ground. I heard another popping sound and then looked up. The young man fell to his knees. He looked at me as blood stained his blonde hair. We stared at each other. His eyes grew dim as the life escaped from his blue eyes. He opened his mouth to say something before I heard the popping sound again. This time his head opened-wide and brain matter hit my face. I was in shock. I was so afraid that I didn't wipe the blood from my face. I turned to find that one of them was still alive. He was moaning and trying to crawl away. Shaking, I looked at him. I couldn't scream. I couldn't do anything. Suddenly, I heard footsteps coming toward us. I turned to see who it was. He was wearing a blue uniform. I looked up to see the shiny gold badge that was sitting on his chest.

"Offi…Offi…Officer….there's someone in the alley shooting people…I don't know… who…where…," I said, stuttering.

He interrupted me. "Are you okay?"

"Ummmm, yes…but somebody is shooting," I said, trembling.

He helped me to my feet. He heard the young man moaning and he turned to look at him. He slowly walked towards him.

The young man looked up. "Thank God…Officer…someone just shot me and my boys."

The cop looked at him. He placed his foot on the young man's chest and pushed. The boy started to scream. "What are you doing?!!"

The cop didn't say anything. He laughed as he reloaded his gun. He pushed his foot deeper into the boy's chest.

"Stop!!!!" he cried out. "What are you doing?" he asked, again, grabbing at the officer's leg.

The officer said, "You have the 'right to remain silent…'"

"Wait…what?" the young man asked.

After he reloaded, he aimed, pulled the trigger and then, *BANG!!!* I stumbled backwards. He walked over to me, extended his hand, smiled and said, "Don't be afraid, Ma'am…I'm the police."

Chapter 1-

The Beginning-

She's gone. Just like that, my life was over. She was everything to me. I prayed to God that he would send me someone – someone to share my life with and as soon as my prayers were answered, the devil took her away from me.

I was in the police academy when I met her. We'd been training together for several months, and I hadn't even noticed her. I was already in several "situations" and wasn't looking to add anyone to my already busy schedule. There was a different one every night. Things were so good that I didn't even bother remembering their names. Their nicknames were whatever day of the week I spent time with them. All I had to do was make sure that I didn't mess up the days of the week and all was good. As long as I didn't call Ms. Monday, Ms. Tuesday or Ms. Wednesday, Ms.

Friday, a brotha stayed out of trouble and the booty kept coming. As I look back, I must admit that I was young and dumb, but I wasn't full of cum, 'cause I was getting it every day – two and three times a day like a doctor wrote a prescription for it. Where I lived, there was no shortage of ass. Females was throwing that shit at a brother like folks throwing candy at a parade. *And who doesn't like candy?*

But then one day, we were doing sit-ups and I was asked to "spot" her. I was holding her feet, counting, and talking to my boy who was spotting someone next to us when, as she came up, I looked at her. I found myself staring into the most beautiful eyes that I'd ever seen. She smiled. After that, I could hear my boy talking, but I was no longer paying attention. Every time she went down to touch the floor, I found myself excited – eagerly waiting for her to come-up again. When she was done, she said, "You can let my feet go."

Snapping out of my daze, I said, "Ummmm, yeah...sure," as I continued to hold her feet.

She smiled. "Ummmmm…any day now…"

Realizing that I was still holding her, I said, "Yeah right…"

She laughed. "I was starting to think you had a gym shoe fetish."

I chuckled. "Naw, but I like what's in the shoes."

"So you have a foot fetish?" she asked, coyly.

"Not at all," I said.

She smiled.

The instructor called for us to do push-ups. She rolled over onto her stomach. I watched her do the first one. As her back arched and her ass rose into the air, she caught me staring.

"Officer Miller, you want to join us?" the instructor called out.

I smiled and slid next to her. We were going at a really good pace until I caught a "Charlie-horse" in my right leg. I fell to the ground. She stopped and crawled over to help me.

"Shit, it's a cramp," I said, grabbing and trying to massage the muscle in my calf. She rubbed her hands together and began to gently rub them over the knot in my leg. "How does that feel?" she asked.

Watching her, come to my rescue, made me completely forget that I was in pain. I wanted to lie to her and tell her that the knot had traveled north to that growing spot between my legs, but I knew that it would be inappropriate. She looked up and smiled. "Is it better?" she asked.

I smiled back. "Yes, it's better."

We stared at each other for what seemed like a lifetime when I broke the silence. "Thank you."

"Do you need some help getting up?" she asked, as she rose to her feet.

The man in me wanted to say, "Hell no," but as I watched the sweat drip from her chin and then roll down the middle of her chest, I said, "Sure…a Brotha can use some help." She stretched out her hand. In that moment, I felt something that I'd never felt before – butterflies. Until that moment, I thought that that shit was a myth, stuff from a fairy tale, a fucking urban legend, but it was real. No other woman made me feel that way and from that moment on, I knew that she was the "one."

I spent every moment doing things to make her smile. My day was incomplete if I didn't see it. Whatever she wanted and needed, I provided, just so that I could see her smile. I couldn't imagine my life without her, so after two months of dating, I proposed to her. She thought that I'd lost my mind. Believe me, I wasn't thinking clearly. It must have had something to do with all of the blood flowing to both of my heads, 'cause in my younger days, I was a dog – trying to sniff every piece of ass that walked passed me. "Love" was a curse word and the thought of spending the rest of my life with just one woman frightened me. My boys used to tease me that one day I would find a woman good enough to fuck "raw" and finally, I did. She made me want to throw it all away – my black book, my condoms, my second phone, everything. She became my "every day" of the week.

I didn't know how I made it this long without it, but I knew that I never wanted to be without it again - love. I remember the day that we got married. I was shaking like a man facing his execution, but when she walked down the aisle wearing that white dress, I knew that I'd made the right decision. It's funny because when I saw her, I cried. I tried to hide the tears, but couldn't. My Best-Man touched my shoulder and said, "You're a lucky man…"

I wiped the tears from my eyes and said, "Thanks, Bruh."

He handed me a handkerchief and said, "Bruh, your mascara is running."

I frowned and took it from his hand. "You got jokes. It's a shame I ain't laughing."

He laughed and said, "Yeah, because you're too busy crying like a bitch."

I frowned, because I was crying like a bitch, but she was worth it. When the preacher said the words, "Until death do you part", I looked at her and said, "You better not leave me."

She smiled and said, "I'm not going anywhere, silly." As her eyes filled with tears, I grabbed her – held her tight in my arms. I didn't wait for the preacher to give me permission to kiss her. I kissed her while promising to never let her go.

And that was it – a beautiful beginning of our lives together. She was my sunrise and my sunset. She was the calm to my storm. She was everything to me. *She was.*

And then it happened…

She was at the store when she called me to find out if we had any pickles and whipped cream.

"Baby…what are you going to do with pickles and whipped cream?" I asked her.

"The baby said that he wanted pickles and whipped cream. Who am I to deny him?" she said, walking through the aisles at the grocery store.

"You and those cravings," I laughed.

"Yeah, I know," she said, moaning.

"What's wrong?" I asked.

"My stomach is getting too big for the baby and this gun on my hip," she said.

"At some point, you're going to have to put in a notice. I don't want anything to happen to my babies," I said.

She giggled. "Your babies will be fine. Let me pay for this stuff so that I can come home to my baby."

And that was the last thing that she said to me.

The next thing I heard was a call come in through the radio that an officer was down. As I heard the address, I wondered if my baby was there securing the scene – maybe arresting the assailant. All that I could think about was my wife and son. I jumped in my car. All the way there, I wondered if they were okay.

When I approached the scene, I noticed that a crowd was gathering. As I worked my way through the people who were there, I was stopped by one of the officers. "I can't let you in there."

"What…why???" I asked, as the panic began to grow inside of me.

"Look…we did everything that we could…" the officer said.

"Man…what the fuck are you talking about? Get out of my way!!!!" I said, trying to push pass him, but he wouldn't budge.

Suddenly, we heard a sound – the sound of tin as it rolled across the concrete. We both looked in its direction as the can of whipped cream made its way into the crowd.

"NOOOOOOOOOOOO!!!!!!" I screamed, pushing him out of the way. I made it through the crowd of officers and Emergency personnel, to find her lying on the ground, dead, a hole where my baby boy once slept, still holding her gun in one hand and the bag with a jar of pickles in the other. I fell to my knees.

"Deborah!!!!!! No, Deborah!!!!!" I said, as I cried uncontrollably. Then, I heard it. Through my agony, my sorrow, and my tears, I heard it - a faint whistle in the darkness. I stood to find out who was doing it or where it was coming from and then as fast as I heard it, it was gone – vanished into the wind.

Chapter 2

After weeks of searching, they caught his ass. Found out that he had a prior rape charge involving a woman and was given seven months in jail. After serving three months, he was released. Once he was on the streets again, he was looking for another victim and he saw her – alone – in the middle of the night – just shopping for foods to appease the little person inside of her. The witness claimed that when she drew her gun, and she asked him to drop his firearm, he fired. Her dying words were, "My baby…my baby!"

And now I sit in court, waiting for this piece of shit to get what's coming to him. After months of waiting for him to be brought to justice, it happened. Worse than the murder of my wife and baby were the words as they were read by the Juror. "Not guilty." I thought that I was having an "out-of-body" experience. "Wait a minute…what the fuck did they say?" I asked the officer sitting next to me.

He looked at me and said, "I think they said, 'Not Guilty."

"Not guilty…What the fuck does that mean? He's a free man? He killed my wife and son. HE KILLED MY WIFE AND SON!!!!!" Before I knew it, I was running towards the front of the courtroom. "You son of a bitch!!! YOU SON OF A BITCH!!!! YOU KILLED MY WIFE!!! YOU KILLED MY BABY!!!"

As they grabbed me to keep me from killing him, he looked at me and smiled. They managed to restrain me and escort me back to my seat. I placed my face into my hands, and cried. "He killed my babies!"

And then I heard it again. As they dragged him out of the courtroom, he whistled. When I looked up in his direction, he stopped, smiled and whistled again as they dragged him down the hall.

And that was it. As the words "Not Guilty" replayed over and over in my head, I felt like I was in a dream – a horrible, horrible dream, but it wasn't. This shit was real. The laws that I'd been hired to uphold had allowed a killer to go free. He got off on some "technicality." *The prosecutor fucked up. He claimed self-defense.* He was given only a few months and a fine for having an unregistered firearm. A fucking slap on the wrist for the lives of two people.

I had to take a leave of absence. I couldn't perform my duties after that. I couldn't eat or sleep. For days, I did nothing but stare at the walls, hoping that I would wake up and find that I'd imagined it all, but it didn't happen. Mourning became a way of life instead of a state of being. It overtook me. I felt like I'd fallen into a hole where no one could find me. Then suddenly, one morning, I woke up, found myself staring at her empty side of the bed and I knew what needed to be done.

Chapter 3~

I found myself watching my calendar and waiting for his release. When that day came, I jumped into my "unmarked" and watched him leave the jail, smiling, just like he did the day that he was acquitted.

I didn't know what or why I followed him. The justice system handed him the sentence that they felt he deserved, but my heart was broken. I was grieving like all of those mothers, fathers, husbands, wives, and children who had lost a loved one. My heart ached as it did when I arrived at a crime scene – standing over the body of someone who didn't deserve to die and like them and the families that loved them, I wanted to know – No, what I needed to know was why? Why her? Why my baby?

As a cop, I wanted him to go to jail for life. As a father and husband, I wanted to take my gun and make him eat it. As a man who believed in the "Word", I wanted balance – "an eye for an eye." I wanted him to be raped like he'd done to all of his victims and then I wanted him to be shot to death and laid out on concrete as people looked on - just like he did to my wife and son. In an ideal world, families of the victims receive justice, the perpetrators of crimes are punished, but the system is flawed and often times, the Devil goes free. I took an oath to uphold the law – not to break it, but what happens when the same laws that keep me from killing him are the same laws that couldn't protect my family, and subsequently let a murderer and rapist go free?

While I contemplated this, I followed him. His first stop was the office of his parole officer. Then, he went to a local bar. Hours later, I watched as he dragged a woman, who was drunk, out of the bar. As she fought him, he dragged her down an alley. I exited my car, walked over, and then stood in the darkness as he ripped her shirt off. She struggled, but was too helpless to fight back. In her weakened state, it was easy for him to overpower her. It was clear that she didn't want this to happen, but was unable to say, "No." He ignored her cries. I couldn't stand to continue to watch this, so I walked out of the shadows and said, "I don't think she wants that."

He released her breast and said, "Who the fuck are you?"

"Let her go," I told him.

"Fuck you…when I'm done, you can have her…if there's anything left," he said, licking her breast.

With tears in her eyes, she mumbled, "Help me."

I pulled my Glock and placed it to the back of his head. "Let her go."

His hands went up in the air. "Okay…okay…letting her go…damn…let's talk about this."

I looked at the woman. She tried to fix her clothing, but was unsuccessful. Tears roll down her cheek.

"Get out of here," I insisted.

She stumbled until she found herself at the end of the alley. Then, she fell to her knees. She needed my help.

Damn. I thought to myself. *This wasn't a part of my plan.* I looked at the man standing in front of me. "Turn around," I instructed.

"Why? What did I do?" he asked.

"What did you do? That's a joke, right?" I asked, not waiting for an answer. I cuffed him and then dragged him down the alley. Once we got to my car, I threw him into the backseat.

"Hey, what the hell are you doing? I didn't do anything wrong…she wanted it…I promise you…she wanted it," he said.

I frowned. "What about this shit screams 'she wanted it?' If she was sober, do you think she would want you? Do you think that she would want you to fuck her in an alley? You lying piece of shit…" I grabbed him by his collar and said, "Get your ass in the car and shut the hell up." I pushed him inside, slammed the door into his face, and then walked over to the young lady who was sleeping peacefully in her own urine. I picked her up and walked her over to my car. I placed her in the front-seat and then buckled her in.

He protested the entire time that he sat in the backseat not realizing what was going to happen to him. I drove around for thirty minutes before I saw a flashing red "vacancy" sign. I pulled up into the parking lot, walked into the office, flashed my badge, paid cash for the room, and then walked back to the car.

"Hey man, you want me to sit in the car while you get your 'rocks' off? Man, that's some bullshit," he yelled from the backseat.

"Shut up," I said.

"Naw, man, I've been locked up too long. I want a piece of that too," he said, slurring his words. "I found her first."

I looked at him. "Shut…the…fuck…up."

He frowned.

I carried the woman into the room and laid her across the bed. She mumbled and reached out to me. "Go to sleep," I told her as she snuggled her face into the pillow.

I walked out of the room and then jumped into the car. I started it and threw it into "drive."

"Damn, that was fast…I guess it's true what they say about cops and their "quick draw"…that shit must have been really good…," he said, laughing.

I looked up at my rearview mirror and saw him smiling back at me. I threw the car in "park" and then walked around to the other side of the car. He was still smiling when I opened the door. "Didn't I tell you to shut the fuck up?"

"Awwwwww man, I was just joking...I've been locked up...just want to have some..."

Before he could finish that sentence he was sucking on the barrel of my gun. "I said, 'shut the fuck up'." Blood began to ooze out of his mouth. I removed the gun.

He spat blood on the floor. I watched as his teeth flew out of his mouth. "Man, you knocked my teeth out."

I shoved the barrel of my gun into his face. "Do I need to tell you again?"

He shook his head. "No."

Now, I was smiling. I kneeled down, collected his teeth and then walked back into the motel room. I placed the teeth in her hand. "A gift," I whispered into her ear. She mumbled and closed her hand.

I walked back outside. He stared at me as he licked his mouth. I jumped back into the car and proceeded to our destination.

I realized as I kept looking into my rearview mirror, that I hadn't really thought this out, but then he did it. Through the few teeth that he had left, he began to whistle. I smiled. While, in the beginning, I wanted to just talk to him, but seeing the man who took the lives of my family, who was in the process of raping another woman, made it clear what needed to be done. He was a virus in need of a cure and I was that cure.

"I have to use the bathroom," he said, quietly.

"What?" I asked, snapping out of my thoughts.

"I gotta piss," he said, raising his voice.

I wanted to tell him to do "it" on himself, but he was in my car and I wasn't cleaning up behind this piece of shit, so I pulled over, walked over to the other side of the car, and then dragged him out of the backseat.

"Thank you...thank you," he said, as I dragged him behind some trees. We walked until we were far away from the road.

"Hey...where are you taking me?" he asked, looking around at his surroundings.

"I thought that we could use some privacy…you know? So you can piss," I said.

"Oh okay…thanks Bro," he said. "I appreciate that. Don't want motherfuckers driving by and looking…" he said.

I frowned. "Yeah, we definitely don't want that."

We walked a little more until we were standing in the middle of some overgrown weeds. Then, he said, "I'm going to need you to un-cuff me or unzip my pants and hold my 'shit' for me."

I ignored what he said and asked, "Why…why did you kill her?"

"Kill who? Come on, man, I really need to piss," he said, squirming.

"Why did you kill my wife?" I asked.

"Your wife? Dude, I don't know what you're talking about…man, I need you to un-cuff me or I'm going to piss on myself."

I pulled my Glock. "I'm going to ask you one more time. Why did you kill my wife?" I asked, placing the gun to his chest.

"Look man…I'm sorry…but I don't know what the fuck you're talking about. Now, if you're not going to un-cuff me at least help me out…I'm begging you, man…"

I reached down between his legs and grabbed him – hard. He screamed, his knees buckled, and he fell to the ground. "Damnit man, what the hell are you doing?" he asked, rolling on the ground.

"Do you still need to piss?" I asked.

"Yeah, man…what the fuck?" he asked, grimacing.

I pointed my gun at him.

He quickly changed his mind. "Naw, man, I'm good…," he said, trying to sit up.

I kneeled down and grabbed him by the face. "You know what the hell I'm talking about."

"No, I don't, man…I wish you would tell me what all of this is about so that I can go home."

I smiled. "You're never going home."

He sat up. "What? Man, this shit has gone on long enough. Now, let me go."

"I'm only going to ask you one more time…"

Trying to hold his hands in the air, he said, "Look, look, look....okay...okay...it was a mistake. You see...she was just at the wrong place at the wrong time...when I saw her leaving the church...in that short skirt...well, one thing led to another...I'm sorry man...I didn't mean to...I'm sick...yeah, I'm sick...I need help."

"Church?" I asked, confused. "What church?"

Now, he looked confused. "You're not talking about the one at the church?"

I shook my head, "No."

"How about the hospital? Was she the one that I did in the hospital's parking lot?"

This motherfucker...I thought to myself. I placed my gun to his forehead.

Suddenly, urine began to stain his pants. "Look what you made me do..." he said.

I ignored him. "Did you know that she was a cop?" I asked.

"Who?" Then suddenly you could tell that something "clicked." Through his drunken haze, he realized what this was all about. He began to laugh before he buckled over and vomited all over himself. He licked his mouth. "Oh her...," he said.

"Yes, her...," I confirmed.

"Look man...you're going to kill me anyway, so I'm going to keep it real." He sighed and then continued, "The bitch was..."

I looked at him. Before I knew it, I hit him, hard, across his face. I tried to slap the taste out of his mouth. "You are talking about my wife..."

He began to laugh.

"And you're right...you are going to die. But before you go, I want to know why? Didn't you see that she was pregnant? Didn't you know that she was a cop?" I asked.

"If you have to ask me why, then you haven't been a cop very long...I did it because I could," he said, matter-of-factly.

Suddenly, everything around me became silent. My heart began to beat so hard that it felt like it was going to pop out of my chest. I looked down at him. I didn't see a man. I didn't see a human. I saw an animal – an animal that needed to be put down. For some odd reason, while looking at him, I began to laugh.

Confused, he said, "What the fuck is so funny?"

I stopped and looked at him. "You…you are fucking funny. Here I am…holding a gun to your head and you have the nerve to talk about killing my wife like it was nothing…like she was nothing…"

He turned up his mouth and said, "Sorry dude, but…"

Before he could finish that sentence, the gun went off.

He screamed. "What the fuck, man? You shot me in my shoulder."

I kneeled down. "Sorry dude…I missed. I meant to shoot you in the head. Let me try that again."

He opened his mouth to say something, but the gun went off again. He screamed. "WHAT THE HELL???!!!! You can't do this shit."

I looked at the hole in his leg and said, "You didn't have to kill her."

"Man, please…I'm begging you," he said.

"Like you said, 'I'm going to kill you anyway.'" I frowned. "But I want you to feel it just like you were going to make that girl feel it in that alley. Like you made my wife and son feel it…"

"Son of a bitch!!!!!" he said, trying to stand. "Look…please…I'm…I'm sorry."

The gun went off again. He screamed. He looked at his other leg. "Please…please… look…please." The gun went off again and this happened several more times until there was only one bullet left.

"Oh my, Gawd…I swe…swear…I didn't mean to, man…I just…I just…"

I mumbled, "Guilty."

"What?" he asked, gurgling and coughing-up blood.

I pressed the gun against his temple and then said, "You are guilty and for taking the lives of two innocent people…your sentence is death."

"Man, they found me not guilty for that," he said.

"Do I look like 'they' to you, motherfucker? You took something from me of great value and now, you have to pay."

He laughed. "You can't do this…you're a cop."

For a moment, I paused to think about that statement. As I stood over his bleeding body, looking at his wounds, I wondered if I was a man who was a cop or a cop who was a man. As the images of her body stretched out across the cold concrete, played in my head, I realized that I was the former. I pulled the trigger one last time. He looked up at me and then a tear rolled down the side of his face. His body went limp and fell to the ground. He was still looking up at me. I removed my handcuffs and then walked away. From that moment on, I didn't see "blue" - just red, but now the "scales" were balanced.

Chapter 4 ~

Chicago 2012

I was sitting at my kitchen table, alone, glancing at the empty chair next to me, sipping from a cup of coffee when I read it. *John Peterman is innocent.* I spit coffee all over my newspaper. I couldn't believe it. As I wiped away the coffee stains to read the rest of the article, I saw it again. *John Peterman, the man accused of murdering Tevin Banks, was found not guilty of second-degree murder and manslaughter.* I stared at it in shock and horror. *How can that be?* That man shot an unarmed teenager in the back four times – not because he did anything wrong but because he looked suspicious. *Damn.* I was at a loss. I still couldn't believe that I was reading this shit. Only in fucking America can this shit happen.

I tried to shake it off. I tried not to let it affect me but how could I ignore this? As a father, as a brother, as a human being? How can I just shrug this off? Another Black male shot and killed simply because he was Black. This shit made no sense to me.

Today, was going to be a rough one. I just knew it. I ironed my clothes, packed my lunch, put on my "blues", my shield and gun and told myself, *You can't let this shit get under your skin. You are a cop. You were hired to serve and protect all people and that's what you are going to do.* I repeated that in my head as I walked towards my car.

My head wasn't in the right place after that. I tried to hide it deep inside but when you hear about that stuff over and over again it's like a wound that isn't allowed to heal. It was Open Season. One after another – a person is killed, not just by gangs, or by the police, but by anyone who has a gun.

Seeing their bodies, lying there, helpless, lifeless - it was a lot; especially when it's all that you do – day in and day out. I remember a time when a murder was so uncommon that when one happened people were actually shocked. Now, it's the other way around. It was like being in a combat zone and the bodies were casualties of war, but this wasn't some Third-world country. This was Chicago.

I tried to think of happy things like thoughts of me and Deborah playing with our son in the park. Then, my loving thoughts were suddenly interrupted when I imagined that while playing with them, John Peterman walked-up behind them and shot them both in the back. I was screaming and crying as I watched their bodies hit the ground and he just stood there, smiling, knowing that there was nothing that I could do other than lock him up.

I was about to pull my gun, but was awakened from my "nightmare" when a car behind me blew its horn. I looked around to find that I was blocking traffic. I needed to pull over. Sweat was pouring from my forehead and my hands were shaking. I stared at them while my thoughts remained trapped in the darkness inside. I took a deep breath and tried to collect myself, but I couldn't get that image out of my head. Their lives, gone in an instant.

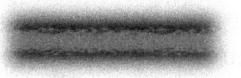

I knew that I should have called in that day – told them that I had the flu or something, but I clocked-in anyway. I needed to find a way to keep my mind on work. That's it and I should be fine, but I couldn't shake the feeling of anger, frustration, and fear. Fear, not for myself but for the ones that I loved and frustration for a system that couldn't protect them.

As I roamed the streets, making sure they were safe, a call came in. *Crime in progress at the corner of Jackson and State…are there any available cars in the area?* I listened to the call. I heard another car respond, but I was right around the corner. I put my foot on the accelerator and arrived at the scene to find a young white male fleeing from the scene. The victim, a young black female lie helpless on the sidewalk. I threw my car into park, jumped out, and ran to her side. She mumbled and pointed towards the perpetrator who was leaving the scene. I looked in his direction and pursued him on foot.

He ran behind some buildings and some parked cars with me hot on his trail until I saw him dash behind some bushes located behind a convenient store. I scanned the area. It was quiet. We were alone. I took out my gun and brushed the bushes - pretending like I couldn't see him.

I smiled and said, "Here kitty, kitty…" I heard the bushes ruffle. I ran my gun over the leaves again. "Here kitty, kitty, kitty…" In the distance, I could hear the sirens approaching. Then, I looked back over at the young lady who was moaning and still lying on the sidewalk. Disgusted, I said, again, "Here Kitty, Kitty, Kitty…" He still didn't come out. *Sigh*. Frustrated and tired of waiting, I said, "Goodbye, Kitty." I pointed my gun into the bushes shot twice and then 'Kitty' stopped moving.

I was walking back towards my car when a fellow officer approached me. "Did you see anything?"

Pretending to be out of breath, I said, "I tried chasing him, but he got away." I looked over and saw another officer assisting the young lady.

"Damn," the other officer said.

"Yeah, I know…he couldn't have gotten that far. He'll turn up. I'm sure of it."

The officer turned to walk away. I looked back over my shoulder at the bushes, smiled, and then walked away.

Chapter 5~

The afternoon was already saying its 'goodbyes' when I'd awaken. I narrowed and strained my eyes to see the clock that was hanging on the wall. *7pm...time to get up.* I struggled to climb out of bed, but duty called.

The room was hot and there wasn't a breeze to be found. As I walked across the room to the bathroom, I tried to remind myself why I didn't need an air conditioner. July in Chicago was called the Killing Season for more than one reason. People die at an alarming rate not only from the senseless violence, but from the heat – the heat was merciless and unforgiving. It did horrible things to people and made people do horrible things to each other.

I walked over to the window to look out into the streets. There was no one. No children laughing and playing, no one on their porches enjoying the summer's night air – there was nothing, absolutely nothing. The area had become a ghost town. People were afraid to come outside. Even with a cop living on the block, they still didn't feel safe.

In the summertime, you could always hear music playing or find someone at the park playing basketball, but not tonight. People weren't coming out tonight. Maybe they knew something that I didn't know. The police are never aware of potential crime. There is a code that the people in the community live by. The police don't usually find out what's going on until it's time to draw the chalk-lines.

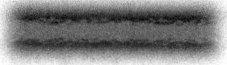

A few nights ago, the streets were filled with people – people laughing and having a good time. Someone must have made a noise complaint because two 'unmarks' came rolling down the street almost mowing down the kids who were jumping rope. When they jumped out, they walked over to where a crowd of boys were listening to some music that was blasting from a vehicle parked on the side of the street. The officer walked over to them and said,

"There was a complaint about the music…I'm going to need you to turn it down."

The three boys started to complain. One of the young men said, "Awwwwww man, we were just listening to some music. We're not hurting anybody."

"I said, turn it down…," the officer said, placing his hands on his belt.

"Okay…okay…okay…" one of the boys said. He leaned in to turn the music down. One of the other boys, reached in his pants pocket for something when all of a sudden the cop yelled, "Gun!!!!" Everyone scattered except for the young man who was still reaching into his pocket. When he looked up, he was staring at the smoking barrel of a gun.

The smell of burnt powder filled the air. When the smoke cleared, the young man closed his eyes as his body fell to the ground. There was a moment of silence before a woman started to scream. Suddenly, a crowd formed. Everyone began to scream and yell at the police officers. The other officer on the scene tried to "contain" the crowd while the officer, who shot the young man, stared at the boy's lifeless body; still pointing his gun at him. I walked over to check the young man's vitals. He was dead. I noticed that the young man still had his hand in his pocket. I reached over to retrieve what was in there to find that there was nothing in it, but a pack of chewing gum.

Shortly afterwards, the paramedics arrived. I watched as the boy's body laid on the concrete. It was so hot that flies began to gather to feed on his flesh. Near the crime scene, you could hear a woman screaming and wailing as someone struggled to keep her from collapsing.

I watched, quietly, as the officers who arrived on the scene talked among each other. Then, I noticed the cop who shot the young man staring at me. He looked at me and nodded. I looked at him and nodded back. It was a silent communication between "brothers" that indicated that the "Blue Code" was being implemented as we built the "Blue Wall" around the crime scene.

When they wrapped-up the crime scene, everyone returned to their homes. I walked over, stood over the blood-soaked concrete, and stared at it. The streets had taken ownership of another life.

Chapter 6

The next day, it was all over the news. *Young Unarmed Black Male Shot by White Cop...* I was listening to the story when all of a sudden the windows of my home began to rattle. I thought that we were having an earthquake until I looked outside to find loud music blasting from a car sitting in front of my house. I looked at the car to see who was sitting in it. I couldn't see their face because there was a cloud of smoke circling their head. I waited to see if someone had called the police because of the disturbance, but nothing happened. The trust between the community and the police had been broken and was now replaced with silence.

In the background, the reporter continued, "...the officer may face charges in two other cases involving excessive force..." I became frustrated, walked over, and turned the TV off. *Not again.* I thought to myself. I was lost in my thoughts until they were interrupted by the glass of water that was vibrating on the kitchen table. I was reminded of the disturbance sitting in front of my house.

I looked over and without thinking, grabbed my gun and shield and headed for the door. When I walked out, there was a green Impala sitting on 22s parked halfway on the street while the other half sat on my lawn. I walked up and then pressed the shield against the window. He rolled down the window. "Can I help you, officer?" exhaling smoke into my face. I scanned the vehicle. He was alone. He was young, white, and covered in tattoos.

"Yeah, you need to turn that shit down and move your car. People don't want to hear that mess." The smell of marijuana filled the air.

He took a long drag on a joint and said, "Dude, I'm just chilling…you should chill too…" He was high as a kite. "You want to hit this?"

I looked at him. "You're smoking that shit in my face?"

He looked at the joint and then said, "Oh this? I got a card for this…you can't do shit about it, dude."

"Let me see the card," I said.

The young man pretended to look for it. "Oh, I must have left it in my other suit," he said, laughing.

"That shit is funny?" I asked.

He continued to laugh. "Yeah...kinda..."

I grimaced and tried to reframe from smacking his ass with the butt of my gun. I took a deep breath and asked, "So, who you over here to see?"

"I'm over here to see my boys...the brothas...my homeboys...my niggas...you know..." he took a drag and then exhaled. "I love these motherfuckers. Do you know that you can get the best shit from over here? These motherfuckers got the hookup." He laughed again. "I just came to get a little, then I'mma go home, fuck my girl, eat some chips, and then sleep all day...you know what I'm saying?" He stuck his hand out to shake mine, but I just looked at it. "Damn...makes my dick hard just thinking about it. Man, that shit right there..." He laughed.

I frowned and then interrupted him. "You're admitting to coming into this community to buy drugs? You know that I can charge you?"

"You could, but you ain't…I'm not 'holding' and all that I have is this joint and it ain't enough for a charge," he said.

The weed or his sense of entitlement was making him cocky, but he was right. I couldn't charge him for a joint, but he was definitely in need of an attitude adjustment.

At first I frowned, figured that I was wasting my time on him when he said, "These niggas got exactly what a motherfucker need…" he laughed again.

I looked at him, smiled, and said, "Hey…look…I got something that you might be interested in."

He took another 'hit' and said, "What you got officer?"

I leaned in and said, "In my house…I got some 'shit' that you might be interested in."

He laughed again, but then became serious. "You got some 'shit'?" he asked.

"Yeah…I got some 'shit'…some of that good shit too," I confirmed.

He looked me up and down and then said, "You dirty?"

I said, "Why don't you come and see?"

He laughed, paused, and looked me up and down. He looked around and said, "Why not…sure…you're a cop. What do I have to worry about?"

I smiled. "Not a damn thing."

He turned off his car and followed me inside.

I sat my gun and shield on the table. "Have a seat…"

"Shit dude…do what you got to do…" He fell onto the couch, grabbed the remote, put his feet on my coffee table, and then turned on the TV.

Look at this motherfucker. I shook my head, walked over, and then closed the blinds. "Give me a second…I'll be back…" I was about to walk away when I said, "You know what? It'll be easier if you come and see the 'shit' instead of me bringing it to you."

He looked around and then asked, "Is it that much?"

I squinted and smiled. "Yeah, it's that much."

He stood and followed me down the hall, laughing all the way. "Maybe after this, we could get something to eat…like some donuts…you like donuts, don't you, Mr. Police Officer?"

I cringed and stopped. He ran into me.

"Dude, sorry about that….where is the shit, anyway?" he asked.

I smiled and said, "It's right in there."

We continued down the dark hallway until we landed in the spare bedroom. He jumped onto the bed and said, "This is some nice shit. You have to be dirty to afford this shit, 'cause I heard that they don't pay y'all nothing. I know brothas flipping burgers making more than you…I bet that shit pisses you off?"

I didn't respond. I walked over to the closet and began to pull a lockbox from the shelf.

He kept talking while I unlocked it. I pulled the 'shit' from the box. He looked up and said, "Wait…what are you doing?"

I smiled and said, "You asked for the 'shit' and I'm going to give it to you." The sunlight bounced off of the steel of the gun.

He scurried away from me. "Naw man, I don't want it…I changed my mind…look…I'mma just get up out of here…"

I laughed. "You come in my neighborhood, making all of that noise, walk up in my house looking for the 'shit'…you find it…now, you don't want it." I shook my head.

"Yeah, yeah…but I change my mind," he said, panicking. "I won't tell anybody…" The young man's face changed as he tried to get away.

"I'm not even worried about that," I confirmed.

He began to cry and plead for his life. "I'm sorry…I'm so sorry."

I looked over at the phone sitting on the nightstand. "Maybe you would like to call the police?"

Confused, he stopped crying and said, "But you're the police…"

Pulling the trigger, I said, "Exactly."

It was a beautiful day for a barbeque. After I cleaned up, I lit up the grill, turned on some music, and listened as the birds sang. As I listened to the meat sizzle on the grill, I thought to myself, *There's nothing like grilled-asshole on a hot summer's day.*

Chapter 7-

I was awakened by the rays of the sun. There was a quiet calm in the air. I yawned and stretched as I thought about my day. I sat up and placed my feet into my slippers and looked up towards the window. Although, the brightness of the sun was blinding, I welcomed the heat. On this day, it didn't matter that it was hot. I almost felt that the heat was necessary because it forced things to move. It caused the truth to expose itself – even the shade couldn't protect you from it.

I jumped into the shower and as the cool water ran down my back, I thought about the man who killed my wife and remembered the look on his face when he realized that he was going to die. Then, I thought back to my wife and wondered what she felt during the last moments of her life. As I remembered the look on his face, I realized that the only thing that mattered is that in the end, he felt her pain and that he felt my pain.

When I was done, I got dressed and then slowly walked down the hallway. I could feel the cold tile beneath my feet. It was quiet – unusually quiet. I walked into my kitchen and turned on the faucet – waiting for the cold water to run hot. As I listened to it circle the drain, I grabbed the coffee can. *This is going to be a two cup kinda day.* I thought to myself. Steam began to fill the sink. I walked the pot over and began to fill it when the silence was broken. *Bang! Bang!* I dropped the pot – glass shattered everywhere. *Shit!* I thought to myself. I was staring at the broken glass when I heard a woman scream. I took a deep breath. Then, I heard her scream again. *This will have to wait.* I walked over to the table, grabbed my gun and keys, and ran out of the house.

I followed the crowd and the screams. Suddenly, a man ran up to me. He stopped me. Speaking frantically, he said, "He looked suspicious…he reached in his pocket…how was I supposed to know that it was a cellphone? How was I supposed to know?" Over his shoulder, I could see a figure twitching on the ground. I pushed the man out of the way and ran to the victim's side. I kneeled down next to him. Blood was oozing out of the hole in his chest. I placed my hands over the wound to try to stop the bleeding, but he was losing too much blood. He grabbed my arm and pulled me closer - towards him. I leaned in. He gurgled as he spoke. "All I was doing was walking down the street...and he shot me...why did he shoot me?"

I looked up and saw the man talking to the other officers who'd just arrived. The young man began to cough up blood. "I was just walking down the street," he said, as his breathing became labored. Suddenly, he coughed and then there was nothing. His eyes rolled up into the back of his head and then he was gone. The EMTs rushed towards me. They began to perform CPR but it was no use. I stopped to speak with the other officers. As we talked, I kept looking back at the body resting on the sidewalk. I then looked over at the man who was telling his version of what happened to everyone who was willing to listen. "It was him or me." I heard him repeat. Then, I remembered what the victim said. "Why did he shoot me?" The man looked at me. I looked back at the body lying on the ground and whispered, "I will get that answer for you."

That night, after a long day of looking at body bags, I walked into my house. A place that was once full of life, love, and laughter was now, empty. I plopped down onto the couch, - sitting in the darkness. I closed my eyes to try to get their faces out of my head. Among them was the face of the woman that I promised that I would protect, but couldn't. The images and their voices flooded my mind. I grabbed my head and shook it, but I realized that that wasn't going to make it go away. There was nothing that I could do, but try to get some rest and pray that I didn't dream. I stood to walk into the kitchen when I heard a crunching sound under my feet. I turned on the light to find the broken glass that was still scattered across the floor. I stared at it as images of dead bodies invaded my mind again. I shook my head to remove them, but their voices called out to me. I grabbed my head and began to scream. I fell to my knees and onto the kitchen floor. I looked at the broken pieces of glass. As I began to pick them up, one of the pieces sliced the side of my hand. I watched as the blood flowed from the wound. I began to cry. I watched as my tears tried to cleanse the wound, but they couldn't. I held my hand close to my chest as I stretched out across the kitchen floor and cried until I fell asleep.

A few hours later, I awakened to find that the glass was still sitting on the floor. I was trying to stand when I noticed the dried blood on my hand and remembered that I'd cut myself. Using the other hand to balance myself, I stood, grabbed the broom, dustpan, and began to sweep up the glass. When I was done, I walked down the hall to the bathroom. I didn't turn on the light because I didn't want to see my reflection in the mirror. I removed my gun from my holster and placed it on the sink. I slowly removed my clothing. Turning on the water, I began to think of her and smile. She used to love taking a shower with me. As I slid under the shower head, I could see her, smiling, as the soap and water covered her growing belly. I remembered the stretchmarks that were forming over her thighs and stomach. I remember telling her how sexy she was as she tried to hide them from me, but I loved her. I didn't care. I knew that the changes in her body were due to her love for me and the little person growing inside of her. As I washed her, I kissed every part of her – grateful for her existence, but now, I stand here alone.

I closed my eyes and allowed the water to run over my head. His words came to me again. "Why did he shoot me?" He didn't say, "Save me." No, he just wanted to know "Why?"

Before my wife was murdered, I'd grown numb to death. I understood that people dying was a consequence of them living. I learned at a very young age that death, by any means, is always tragic, but sadly, a necessary part of life. We all have an expiration date, but it is those who expire too soon that leave us broken, angry, and confused.

Chapter 8 ~

I was only eight when I found him. Things were tight and my dad struggled to keep food on the table. My mother and father fought everyday as they had to choose between keeping our bellies full and having to keep a roof over our heads. Many times, they chose the latter. I remember the sleepless nights because the hunger kept us awake. If you've never been hungry, you wouldn't understand, but it felt like your stomach was trying to eat itself. There were some nights that the hunger was so unbearable that I ate the roaches to keep the pain away. Many days we survived on powdered milk, moldy bread, and government cheese. Sometimes, we were lucky and we would get peanut butter from the food pantries. It was on those days that I felt like the luckiest kid in the world, but something about not being able to feed his kids, tore at my father. Many nights, I would find him in the darkness, crying.

"Daddy, what's wrong?" I asked.

He wiped his face and asked, "What are you doing out of bed?"

"I can't sleep," I said, as I began to climb into his lap.

He kissed my forehead. "I can't sleep either," he said.

I snuggled deeply into his arms and said, "Why can't you sleep, daddy?"

He looked at me. "You're too young to understand."

I smiled. "I'm a big boy, daddy. I can count all the way to a hundred."

He laughed. "Well, I guess that makes you a big boy."

I smiled.

He continued. "When I grew up, I had dreams to do so many things, but then I met your mother…"

I frowned.

"No, I'm not saying that meeting your mother was a bad thing…it's just that…with love comes a lot of responsibility. Then, we had you guys and…" he paused to look at me. "Well, things didn't turn out as planned."

Confused, I asked, "You love us…don't you, daddy?"

He responded, "I love you more than life itself…that is why it is so hard to watch you suffer because of the decisions that I made."

I wrapped my arms around his shoulders. "Awwwww, daddy…it's not that bad. I like cheese sandwiches. After a while, they mess up your tummy, but…" I smiled. "I get to eat them with you." I looked up to find that my daddy's eyes were filled with tears. "Did I say something wrong?"

He wiped his face on his sleeve and said, "No, son."

"Is everything going to be okay, daddy?" I asked.

He stared at me for a long time before saying, "Everything is going to be just fine, son…now, go to bed."

I climbed out of his lap. I was walking towards the door when I looked back and said, "Goodnight, daddy."

"Goodnight, son," he said, looking out into the moonlight.

The next morning, we all jumped out of our beds and ran down the hall. As we all stood in the living room's door, we saw his feet dangling in the air. As our eyes slowly looked up, we saw the rest of him, swinging from a rope that he'd tied to the ceiling fan.

That day, I learned a lot of valuables lessons, but the one that sticks with me is that a man knows when enough is enough. A man must be in control of his destiny – from beginning to end and while we may not like his choices, we must respect it. He couldn't end our suffering and didn't want to continue to watch it. I will always love and respect him for that. But sadly, it didn't change anything. After his passing, things only got worse.

Before the dirt settled around his casket, my mother was sweating-up the sheets with another man. We didn't go hungry again after he moved in, but the price that my mother had to pay to keep our bellies full was great.

Something about him wasn't right. He was an asshole and because he kept the lights on, he felt like we owed him something. He was always calling us out of our names and picking on us for no reason. My mother tried to make us call him "Daddy", but I wasn't going to do that. I had one daddy and he, according to my mother, was on his way to Heaven.

You could hear them going at it every night whether she wanted to or not. She would beg and plead for him to stop, but he wouldn't until one day, we made the decision to make him stop.

For months, we saw the bruises. For months, we heard the cries and then one night, my brother, Abel, and I decided to put an end to it. One night, we waited until the "banging" stopped and when we thought that the close was clear, we entered the bedroom. We could hear her whimpering from behind the bathroom door. He was resting peacefully on my mother's side of the bed with a belt in his hand. My brother and I stood over him – watching his chest as he inhaled and exhaled. We looked at each other. I took the belt from his hand. He began to stir. "Bitch… you gon' learn today," he mumbled. We looked at each other again. My brother walked over and took a pillow from my father's side of the bed. When he walked back over, he held the pillow and then nodded his head. I took the belt and slid it behind his neck. When it came around, I buckled it around his neck and pulled it. He jumped up, grabbing at his neck. He struggled. My brother jumped on top of him and placed the pillow on his face. I pulled the belt tighter as my brother pushed the pillow into his face. He pushed and I pulled. Again, he pushed and I pulled until finally, he stopped moving. We didn't want to take any chances, so we continued to pull and push until my brother looked at me and said, "He's done."

I removed the belt and placed it back in his hand. On our way out of the room, we put my father's pillow back on his side of the bed and exited the room – gently, closing the door behind us. We were lying in our beds when we heard a scream coming from my parent's bedroom.

"Oh my Gawd…nooooooooo!!!!!!!" she said.

My brother and I looked at each other, smiled, and then fell asleep.

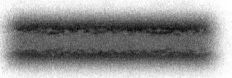

They investigated the "public service." My brother was sent to "juvy", but I was never implicated. When everything went down, he decided that I deserved a chance to have a future that didn't involve chains, steel bars, and becoming somebody's girlfriend. Like our father, he'd decided that I'd suffered enough so while his freedom was taken, he allowed me to keep mine and I went on to become a police officer.

Chapter 9 -

The 4th of July

As I sat in my "unmark" watching everyone in the park barbequing and having a good time, I couldn't help but think about all of the officers who were working that day, away from their families, to keep the streets safe. As I thought about this I heard the laughter of a little boy as he played with his father. I heard the man tell the little boy, "Come on, son…you can do it." My thoughts drifted to my unborn child and what life would have been like if he'd survived. Then suddenly my thoughts were taken back to the day that I saw my dad, hanging from the ceiling - his body swinging back and forth. I closed my eyes to try to erase the image from my mind when my thoughts were interrupted by a knock on the car's window.

"Would you like something cold to drink," she asked.

I jumped up and found myself peering down the blouse of a woman who clearly thought that today was a "bra-optional" day. Then, my eyes traveled "north" to a face that contained the most beautiful smile that I'd seen in a long time. I rolled down the window.

She asked again. "Would you like something cold to drink?"

For a few seconds, I stared at her mouth and wondered what she tasted like. I became warm and uncomfortable. I adjusted myself in my seat before saying, "Sure, I would like something to drink."

She smiled as she strolled away from the car. I'm not sure if she was doing it on purpose, but she moved her hips and her ass, in a way that spoke to me. It reminded me how long it'd been since I'd made love to anything other than the palm of my hand. She bent over to grab a bottle of water from the cooler. She turned and caught me staring. She licked her lips as she walked back towards me. She leaned into the car.

"Here you go, Officer," she said, smiling.

I took the bottle from her and opened it. I took a drink and swallowed – hard.

She smiled. "Somebody is thirsty."

I smiled. "Somebody's real thirsty."

She smiled, again. "And how thirsty are you?"

"Real…fucking…thirsty," I confirmed.

We both began to laugh. She held out her hand.

"My name is Candy," she said.

I took her hand. "Is that your street name or the name on your Birth Certificate?"

She laughed. "It's the name on my Birth Certificate."

I smiled. "Candy….that won't be hard to remember because I like candy."

She laughed and said, "Who doesn't?" She looked at my badge. "So you're Officer C. Miller. What does the 'C' stand for?"

I looked at her mouth and wanted to say something 'dirty', but decided against it. "It stands for Cain."

"Well, Officer Cain Miller, it's really nice to meet you."

"Same here," I said, putting the bottle to my mouth.

A bead of sweat rolled down her neck into her cleavage. She caught me staring, again. I looked up and she was smiling. "Well, I better get back before I burn the food."

"Yeah, we wouldn't want that," I said.

She reached into my car, passed the rifle that was sitting next to me, and grabbed a pen that was sitting in the cup holder. She took my hand and began to write something inside of it. When she was done, she folded my hand over the pen and said, "For the next time you're thirsty."

She smiled and walked away. I opened my hand to find her name, her phone number, and a "smiley face."

I smiled as I watched her walk away.

The noise wouldn't let me sleep. I couldn't tell the difference between the gun shots and the firecrackers. I could have easily stopped the noise, but who wanted to be the asshole who wrote tickets on the Fourth of July. I was staring at the ceiling when I remembered Ms. Candy. I reached over to turn on the light and realized that I'd washed my hands only leaving a trace of the message behind. I grabbed my phone and tried deciphering what was left of the message. After three calls to complete strangers, I decided to try one last time. The phone rang five times, I was about to hang up when suddenly I heard a voice. Sleepily, she said, "Hello."

Nervously, I cleared my throat and said, "I'm thirsty."

Groggily, she giggled and said, "Me too."

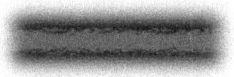

It was 3am when she walked through my door. She was wearing a trench coat and a pair of gym shoes. Her hair was tussled from sleeping on it. She looked at me and said, "Where's your bedroom?"

I smiled, raised an eyebrow, and then pointed down the hall. She removed her coat, exposing a black teddy that was wrapped tightly around her skin. She walked over and took my hand. We walked down the hall to my bedroom. She looked at the bed. She could tell from the dents in the mattress that someone had slept on both sides of the bed. "Will your girl be home soon?" she asked.

I looked at the bed and then I looked back at her. "No, she won't be coming home soon."

She stared at me for a second before taking my hand and walking over to the bed. We both climbed in and fell fast asleep.

Chapter 10~

I awakened to find her resting peacefully in my arms. I could feel her heart beating against my rib cage. The heat of her body reminded me of my loneliness. It had been so long since I'd let someone "inside" that I didn't want to let her go. I could feel myself "growing" under the blanket. I wanted to spread her legs and climb inside of her, but I decided that as much as I wanted her, I just couldn't; not right now. There will come a time, soon enough, but until then, a cold shower would just have to do.

I gently removed her arms, reached over, placed my gun in the drawer, and then locked it. Sitting on the edge of the bed, I looked at her. She grabbed a pillow and nuzzled her face inside of it. I began to walk out of the room when I looked back again at the woman sleeping in my bed. For a moment, I began to feel guilty. Her presence in my life so soon after my wife's and baby's death was a violation, but I hadn't realized how lonely I was until I held her in my arms. I needed somebody. Who? I wasn't sure, but I knew that I needed somebody.

I walked into the bathroom and began to relieve myself. After flushing the toilet, I walked over to the sink to wash my hands. I looked up at the mirror. The eyes looking back at me belonged to a different man. They were tired – tired of all of the bullshit. Then, I remembered the young man, holding my hand, and looking up at me. My thoughts were interrupted when there was a knock on the door.

"Yes…I'll be out in a second…" I said, removing my clothing. Before I could put a 'period' on the end of the sentence, the knob on the door began to turn. She looked in. "Would you like for me to make us breakfast?"

Naked and confused, I said, "Huh?"

"Eat…you know…food?" she said, as she took inventory of my body.

Not really sure what to say to her, I just said, "Yes?"

She smiled and said, "Good."

I turned and stared at the reflection looking back at me. I smiled and said, "It's good...enjoy it."

After I took a quick shower, I dressed, and walked down the hall. Watching her move around in that Black teddy was making me horny. I needed a distraction, so I sat down and opened up the newspaper to take my mind off of the growing urge inside of me. She made some ham, eggs, and toast. She walked over and poured me some coffee.

"I'm sorry, but there wasn't much in the fridge. I cooked what you had in there. Except for whatever that was sitting wayyyyyy in the back...I think it might have waved at me," she laughed.

It might have. I thought to myself – remembering the dead asshole who came into my house, the other day, looking for the 'shit'. I sipped the coffee. "Thank you...I appreciate this."

She sipped from her cup. "Soooooooo... where's the woman of the house?" she asked.

I looked down at the cup.

"I'm sorry...I shouldn't have asked you about your business," she said.

We were quiet for a minute when she said, "I noticed the nursery..."

I looked up at her.

"Sorry...minding your business again," she said, taking a bite out of the toast.

I think that she figured out that I wasn't the "sharing" type, so we remained quiet for the remainder of breakfast.

When we were done, I stood to take the plates away.

"No, let me do it," she said, taking the plates from my hand.

I watched her as she raked the remaining food from the plates into the garbage.

"So...do you make it a habit of running around Chicago...half-naked...sleeping in strange men's beds...making breakfast for them?" I asked.

She smiled. "Naw, but there's something about you...I feel like we've met before...maybe in another life. Plus, you're a cop. What would you possibly do to me?"

You'd be amazed at what I would do to you. I thought to myself. "You're right…what would I do to you?"

"Yep, you wouldn't hurt a fly," she said.

I frowned. "Yes, I would…I hate flies. Flies are maggots with wings. I kill flies and I kill maggots." I said.

She smiled. "When I said 'fly', I meant people and that you wouldn't hurt them."

I smiled and said, "I knew what you meant and when I said that I hated them, flies and maggots, and that I would kill them, I meant 'people' too."

There was a moment of uncomfortable silence. She walked up, threw her arms around my neck, and said, "Stop trying to be mean when you know that you're nice…"

"Nice until I'm not…" I said, looking deep into her eyes.

Chapter 11-

It was a beautiful Thursday morning. I was cruising down Michigan Avenue when I saw two people standing on the corner. When they saw me approaching, they walked away from each other – in two different directions. I pulled up to one of them. *Don't run, motherfucker...don't run.* I thought to myself. And what did he do? He ran. *Sigh.* "It's too hot for this shit," I mumbled, as I got out of the car. I chased him on foot and down the street. Because there was so much pedestrian traffic, he managed to evade me. Suddenly, he was gone. I'd lost him. When I finally made it around the corner, I found myself standing in the middle of the street – alone.

I looked around and found an abandoned building. I pulled my Glock and slowly approached it. As I walked around the building, I saw that someone had removed one of the pieces of wood that covered one of the doors. I pushed the door and walked in.

I traveled down the hall, kicking discarded syringes, as I navigated from room to room until I came upon one of the bedrooms.

I walked in, looked around, opened the closet, found no one, and then walked out of the room. I repeated this two more times until I came upon the last bedroom. As I approached the door, I noticed a shadow standing behind it. I kicked the door hard causing it to hit whatever or whoever was standing behind it.

"Ouch!!!! Son of a bitch…," he said.

I walked in and snatched him from behind the door.

Trying to catch the blood that was streaming down his face, he said, "You broke my damn nose."

I threw him onto the floor. "Who told you to run?"

"I saw a strange man looking at me…shit, I didn't know what you wanted…could have been a damn bill collector."

"Or it could have been a fucking cop," I said, as I searched his pockets.

"Hey…you have to have Probable Cause for that shit…" he said, still holding his nose.

"I'm doing this CAUSE I fucking feel like it. BeCAUSE you're PROBABLY a fucking drug dealer," I said, pulling three bags out of his pockets. "Well, there goes the PROBABLE part…Is this what I think it is?"

Frowning, he said, "I guess it depends on what you think it is."

I shoved my gun in his face. "I THINK it's fucking drugs, asshole. Are you trying to get smart?"

Stuttering, he said, "Naw…naw…I wasn't trying to do that."

I removed the gun and said, "I'm going to ask you again…what…is…this?"

"Man, you already know what it is…I'm not gon' to incriminate myself," he said.

I began to laugh. "Dude…if your ass wasn't so fucking stupid you would realize that these bags that I just pulled out of your pocket 'incriminates' you."

The young man smiled and said, "OR I can say that you planted them on me….it'll be my word against yours."

We were now staring at each other in an empty abandoned building. I looked at him and smiled. "Wait here."

"Man, you better take me in…I'm not waiting for shit."

I listened as he protested until I found what I was looking for and then walked back into the room.

When I came back, he looked at me. "What you gon' do with that?"

I smiled. "I'm going to give you a taste of your own medicine."

"Man, you ain't giving me shit. You better let me go…I'm already gon' get rich off of this broken nose…Anything else that you do to me would be like the cherry on top…"

I looked at him. "You know…I was going to make this easy for you, but…" I poured the contents of the bag into the palm of my hand. He tried pushing away from me, but he wasn't going anywhere. "Come on, MAN…I'm gonna fix that nose for you."

"Stop…stop…stop this shit…!!!!" he shouted, as I placed my palm over his nose.

He grabbed at my hands. "Now, see…here I am trying to fix your nose and you're resisting and the first thing that y'all scream is police brutality." I shook my head. "Ungrateful bastard…" He continued to struggle. I held him as he inhaled a few more times, twitched, and then there was nothing.

I looked at the needle that was sitting next to him. *Such a waste. We could have had so much fun. Oh well.* I thought before letting myself out.

It'd been a long day. All I wanted to do was go home and get some rest. I was turning the corner to my block when a call came in about a domestic disturbance. The disturbance was only four blocks away, so I decided to stop by and check it out. I radioed in that I would handle it and proceeded to the address. When I arrived, I rang the doorbell. The "man" of the house answered the door.

I peered into the house over his shoulder. I could see three kids and a woman who were visibly beaten.

"How can I help you, Officer?" he asked.

"We got a call involving a domestic violence situation...," I said, taking note of his size. He was a big man, but not too big for the Glock that was sitting on my waist.

He interrupted me. "One of the kids accidentally called you...believe me...it won't happen again."

"Oh...that's what happened?" I asked.

He sucked his teeth. "Yep, that's what happened."

Looking over his shoulder, I said, "I'm going to need to talk to the child who made the call."

He leaned into my face. His breath wreaked of alcohol. "Like I said...he made a mistake."

I leaned towards him and said, "I'm not leaving until I talk to the child." I placed my hand on my gun.

He looked down at my hand and then back over his shoulder, "Tommy...bring your ass here and tell this man what he wants to hear so that I can get back to my game."

Slowly, a little boy approached the door. The man grabbed his shoulder and began to squeeze it. "Tell...him...that...it...was...a... mistake."

The little boy looked up. With tears rolling around the blue ring that wrapped itself around his eye, he said, "Yep...it was..." He paused, looked at the man, and continued, "...a mistake."

The man looked at me and smiled. "See, I told you."

I kneeled down to look at the boy. "What happened to your eye?"

The man tightened his grip on the boy's shoulder. The boy looked up at the man. "Ummmmm…I fell. That's it…I fell."

I smiled. "You fell?"

The little boy, confirmed, "Yep, I fell."

I stood up, looked the man in his eyes, and asked, "He fell?"

"Didn't he say that he fell?" he said, frowning.

"I need to check the rest of your family to make sure that nobody else fell," I said.

"First, I ain't got to let you do shit. Second…" he said, now sticking his finger into my chest. He continued, "…I SAID that they are okay."

I grabbed his finger and twisted it until it was sitting in the middle of his back.

He began to scream. "What the fuck, man?"

I pushed my way into the home. The woman and the children were cowering in the corner. I slammed the door and locked it behind me.

"Are you okay?" I asked, them.

They looked in the man's direction and said, "Yes…ummmmmm…yes…we're okay."

I dragged him over to them and said, "Look at this shit. Does that look okay to you?"

"Yes…" he started to say before I twisted his arm and the truth came out. "No…no…it doesn't."

I let him go.

"Hey…this is some bullshit. You can't do this. If she doesn't file a complaint then you have to leave," the man said.

I kneeled down and looked at him. "I could just leave, but what would you learn from that?" I asked.

He pushed back away from me. "Huh? What are you talking about?"

I smiled and walked into the living room and sat down in front of the TV. "What are we watching?"

The man stood and then walked in the room. "Look…I think you should leave."

I pulled my gun from my holster and then placed it on the table. "Ask the young lady to come in here."

He looked confused, but turned and said, "Alice…get your ass in here."

Alice walked into the room.

I looked at her. "Alice…I'm going to need you to go back out…he needs to learn how to call you like you deserved to be called…Now, Alice, could you please leave the room?" I asked.

Confused, she looked at him like she was waiting for his permission. I looked at him. He nodded his head and then she walked out of the room. "Now, do the shit again and this time act like she's a woman who deserves respect…and I'm only going to ask you to do it once…" I paused and looked over at the television. "…looks like the game is in half-time, so I would like this lesson to be short."

The man frowned. "I ain't doing…"

Before he could finish the sentence, my fist was in his throat. He fell to his knees – gasping for air. "Now, you were saying?" I asked.

When he was able to catch his breath, he said, "Alice…Alice…could you please…"

I interrupted him. "I need you to put some 'love' on the word, 'please.'" I walked back towards the couch.

"The fuck?" he asked.

"Am I going to have to come back over there?" I asked.

Rubbing his throat, he said, "No."

"Now, you were saying?" I said.

He began. "Alice, could you please…"

"PLEASE," I said.

"Alice, could you PLEASE come in here?" he asked, nicely.

Alice walked in the room, smiling. I looked at her. "Thank you, Alice, for joining us. Now, Alice, do you have anything that I could eat while I watch the game?"

She looked at me and said, "Well, I made him a sandwich."

I looked at her. "Is there any poison in that sandwich?"

She looked over her shoulder and said, "Not this one." She turned back towards me and smiled.

I put my feet on the table and said, "I would like to have that sandwich and something cold to drink…could you PLEASE, Alice?"
She looked over her shoulder and then back at me and said, "Yes, you may…give me a sec."

I smiled and said, "Thank you, Alice."
The man frowned at me. When she re-entered the room, I said, "Thanks again." I took a bite out of the sandwich. "Oh my goodness, Alice. This sandwich is absolutely delicious…tastes like an angel made it."

She smiled through the cuts and bruises on her face and said, "Thank you." A tear rolled down her cheek.

I swallowed and said, "Alice, could you please have the kids come in here for a second?"

She smiled and said, "Sure."

She grabbed the kids and then re-entered the room. I looked at them – all battered, beaten, and afraid of the monster sitting across from them. I looked at her and was reminded of my mother. She didn't deserve this – no woman, child, or human being deserved this. I reached for one of the kids. "Little One…could you please hand me the remote?" The child happily walked away and then returned with the remote in his hand. I turned down the volume on the TV. "Now, we have a situation here. We have a man who needs to be taught a lesson. Now, I could take him to jail, but he'll call Alice, crying like the bitch that he is, she will most likely bail him out, and then before you know it, he'll be right back to kicking your asses before she could get the key out of the door or he could learn something really valuable today and I think it would be better taught by the people who've experience it." I paused to look at them. Attentively, they listened. "You guys will make a better teacher than some jail-cell." They all looked confused as I continued, "Now, I don't want you to tell me what he did to you...what I want you to do is gather all of the things that he has used to beat you and I want you to bring it in here and put it on this table." Perplexed, they all looked at me. "Think about it...now, hurry up...the game is about to come back on." They looked at each other and then began to run around the house. Moments later, they all returned to the room. The first one threw a shoe and a belt on the table. The second one, threw a broom and a brush on the table. The third one, threw an electrical cord and a ruler on the table and then their mother entered the room. She placed some handcuffs, a lighter and a pack of cigarettes on the table. I looked at her. She opened her blouse to reveal all of the burn marks on her chest. I looked over at him and said, "You are the lowest..."

"Look...look...I've been out of work. I'm stressed and she won't control those damn kids and she don't have sex with me when I want to and..."

I stood, grabbed my cuffs, and walked over to where he was sitting. "It's okay...I understand," I said.

"You understand?" he asked.

I grabbed his hands and placed the handcuffs on them. "Yes...I do. That is why this moment in your life is so important. It's definitely going to change you. I like to call it my version of 'Get Right.'"

"Get right?" he asked.

"Yes...get right...you gon' get right because you've been getting it wrong."

"Man, look...I promise you. It will never happen again," he said.

I laughed. "Of course it won't..." I began to remove his clothing. I pulled his shirt over his head and then wrapped it around the cuffs. Then, I removed his pants and underwear.

"Hey, what the fuck are you doing?" he asked.

The kids began to laugh.

"I see why she doesn't want to have sex with you…" I shook my head. "It's always the little dick motherfuckers with all of the anger…"
I took the other pair of cuffs from the table and then placed them on his ankles.

"Hey…what the fuck are you doing?" he asked again.

"Me? Oh, I'm going to go and eat your sandwich and watch the rest of this game. Now, them? They are going to beat the shit out of you until I tell them to stop."

Everyone in the room except for me, said, "WHAT????!!!!!"

I plopped down on the couch and said, "Yep…now, take this shit off of the table and get started." Having me there to protect them gave them a sense of power that they hadn't had in a long time. They grabbed that stuff from the table so fast that even I was impressed. They all took turns hitting him. He screamed and begged for them to stop, but they ignored him. I turned up the volume and began to eat my sandwich.

When the game was over, I looked over to find him beaten until his face was swollen. I looked on the floor and noticed that there was a bat lying next to him.

"Who added the bat?" I asked.

The youngest child, raised his hand like he was in school and said, "ME!!!"

I smiled and said, "Nice touch."

The little boy smiled, proudly. I looked at the man who was now crying and said, "Something is missing." I looked over at the table and noticed that the lighter and the cigarettes were still sitting on it. I looked at Alice and said, "Come on...you can do it."

She looked down at the man, walked over to the table, lit two of the cigarettes and then proceeded to place it against his skin. He screamed. "Stop!!!! Nooooooo....Stop!!!!"

I walked over and lit the rest of the cigarettes and then gave them to the kids. "Go ahead...it's okay."

They looked at him and then proceeded to burn his skin. "Noooooooooo….pleeeeeeaaaaase!"

This went on for a few more minutes until I felt that he'd had enough. I was getting ready to leave, but felt like something else was missing. I asked, "What hand does he beat you with?"

They all yelled, "HIS RIGHT-HAND!!!!"

I looked at Alice and said, "Let's make sure that this never happens again." Alice turned to her kids. The looks on their faces cried out to her, then she turned and looked at me. She walked outside and then returned with an ax.

He saw her walk back in. "NO! WAIT! WHAT ARE YOU DOING?!!!! YOU CAN"T DO THIS!"

I pinned his hand to the floor. Alice raised the ax over her head.

"Stop!!!!!" He yelled. "Alice…please I'm begging you…don't do this. Alice, baby, I love you."

Alice looked at her kids and then back at me.

"BITCH...YOU BETTER NOT...I'M TELLING YOU...YOU DO THIS AND I WILL FUCKING KILL YOU!!!!" He said, yelling.

Alice smiled. "You can't kill anybody with no hands." Alice nodded and with one swing, the "tool" that was used to victimize them for so long was now sitting on the living room floor.

"Oh my Gawd...no, you didn't...Oh my Gawd...my hand...my hand!!!!!!" he yelled.

I looked at Alice. "Look at you...I'm so proud of you." Covered in blood, she smiled.

"I'm sorry...I'm sorry....I'M SORRY!!!!" he begged.

"Well, look at that. I would say that he passed this class with a flying hand...I meant 'colors'...flying colors. Wouldn't you agree?"

They all nodded, "Yes."

He looked at me. Whimpering, he said, "You did this."

I looked around the room and said, "I didn't do anything. I responded to a call of domestic violence where a woman and kids defended themselves against their attacker."

"You BITCH!!!!" He cried. "I can't believe you did that."

I shook my head. "There is nothing worse than a wife-beater who screams like a bitch," I said, disgusted.

Alice smiled as she wiped blood on her dress.

I kneeled down beside him and removed my handcuff from the remaining hand. "Now…you see…I didn't do any of this…I just created an atmosphere that was conducive to learning." I turned to the kids and asked, "Did anyone see me do anything?"

They all responded. "NO!!!!"

"Now, don't you all feel better…I don't know about you, but I do," I said, looking at them. They all smiled and nodded their heads.

Then, I looked back at him. He was in shock. "If I have to come back over here, it's gon' be your ass." I looked at Alice and the kids. "Now, call the medics. He looks like he learned his lesson." I walked over to the door. "You all have a good day."

The youngest child, said, "Thank you" as I walked out of the house, closing the door behind me.

I was on my way back home when another call came in. "Officer is in need of assistance…" *Shit.* I thought to myself. *This bullshit never stops.* I turned my car around and responded to the call. When I arrived at the scene, I saw an officer sitting on top of a young girl. He looked up at me. "She's resisting arrest…get her feet!"

I looked at the girl who looked like she was barely 100 pounds soaking wet. He was 400 pounds and a Thanksgiving dinner with all of the trimmings away from 500. He was crushing her.

"Please get him off of me. I can't breathe...I can't breathe," she said, begging.

I frowned. "What are you doing? This is a child," I said.

"A child that stole some cigarettes from that store over there," he said, trying to handcuff her. "Now, help me..."

I folded my arms and asked, "You're sitting on that child's back over some cigarettes?"

"Look, if you're not going to help..." Suddenly, he pulled out his Taser. He pointed it at her back and pulled the trigger. She screamed. I looked around.

A crowd was forming. I kneeled down and held her hands. He placed the cuffs on her and then pulled her up by her hair. The little girl screamed. He dragged her to the car and then threw her in the back seat. She hit her head on the doorframe – knocking her out.

Winded, he looked at me and said, "Thanks brother...I got it from here." He patted me on the shoulder. I looked at his hand and then at the unconscious little girl lying on the back seat.

I walked over to my car and watched as he pulled away. I was going to turn around and go home, but decided to follow him instead. We were a few blocks away from the precinct when I threw on my lights. The car pulled over.

I stopped my car and then approached his. "Hey brother," he said, breathing heavily. "You forget something?"

The young lady began to stir. I looked at him. "Hey, I need you check your trunk…"

He frowned. "Bro, I can look at that at the 'house.' You didn't have to stop me for that."

I looked over to the passenger seat of his car where a half-eaten six piece and some fries were sitting.

She was waking up. "Really, you have to see this…" I said.

He smiled, wiped his hands on his clothes, and said, "It must be important to stop me…"

"Oh, it is," I said, walking to the back of the car.

He followed behind me. "Pop it, brother," I said.

He popped the trunk and then it flew open. "Now, what's the problem?" he asked.

I pointed to the plates. "See…it's right there."

He kneeled down. "What…where?"

I pointed. "Right there."

He kneeled closer. I looked around before I pushed him inside.

Shocked, he said, "What the fuck, man? Stop playing." He tried climbing out.

I grabbed his Taser, pointed it, and then pulled the trigger. He stuttered in agony. "What…the…fuck…are…you…doing?"

"How does that feel?" I asked. I held the trigger and he continued to scream. "Noooooooooooo!!!" Suddenly, he grabbed his chest. I stopped. Reaching out to me, he said, "My chest. I…think…I'm…having…a… heart…attack."

I turned and walked back to the side of the car where the girl was now sitting. I opened the door. "Come on," I said, taking her hand.

"Huh?" she mumbled.

"I need your help," I said.

She climbed out of the car and followed me to the back of the car. We both looked at him. Confused, she looked at me.

"Should we let him die?" I asked.

He reached out to her, gasping for air, he begged, "Please...help me." His eyes were bulging out of his head. "I can't breathe....I can't breathe." She frowned and moved away from him.

"Come on...we don't have all day," I said, looking around.

He reached out for her again. She looked back at me. "Yes," she said. "We should."

I smiled. "Then help me get him back in the front seat."

We both struggled to pull him out. We dragged him to the driver's side of the car, opened the car door, and sat him inside.

"Please...I think I'm dying," he said, reaching out to us. "Call for help..."

I looked down at the little girl. She looked up at me. We both watched him struggle to breathe. He grabbed his chest one last time and then there was nothing. I closed the car door and then looked at her. "Run...I got it from here." She took off running to the other side of the street.

By the time that the paramedics arrived, I'd already "swept" the crime scene. When they asked what happened. I shrugged my shoulders and said, "Looks like he had a heart attack."

The paramedic looked at me and said, "Damn, if only you'd got here sooner. You could have probably saved his life."

I smiled and looked at the little girl who was watching the situation from a distance. She waved. I nodded my head and said, "If only..."

Chapter 12~

When I pulled up, she was waiting for me. She jumped out of the car, smiling and waving. "Hey you," she said.

I looked at her. "What brings you here?" I asked.

"You, silly?" she asked.

"Me...is that so?" I asked.

"Yes, it's so....I just thought that I would stop by...maybe see if you were hungry or maybe thirsty," she said, laughing.

I smiled. "Well, I did just have a sandwich, but I guess I could use a little something," I said.

"Good," she said, as she sashayed back to her car. She reached inside of her car and grabbed a picnic basket that was sitting on her seat. She closed her door. "Can I get some help?"

Curiously, I walked over and took the basket from her hand. "Who do you think is about to sit in a park...in Chicago? I'm a cop and I'm not trying to do that."

She looked stumped. "Well, we can put a blanket on your floor and eat it there. If that would make you feel safe."

"Ummmmmm sure...what is this anyway and why?" I looked at the basket.

"I kinda felt sorry for you...after looking in your refrigerator...looks like you could use a decent meal," she said, walking towards my front door.

"So...you just felt like feeding a brotha?" I asked, putting my key into the door.

"I like you, Officer...is there something wrong with that," she said, walking inside.

I watched her as she walked passed me. "No, there's nothing wrong with that."

I sat the basket down on the floor and walked in the back to grab a sheet. When I came back, she was barefoot and lying on the floor. I put the sheet down and she grabbed the basket. She opened it, placing some fruit, cheese, crackers and a bottle of wine on the floor.

"Do you have any glasses?" she asked.

I stood to walk into the kitchen. I opened the cabinet and saw the champagne glasses that Deborah and I drank from on our wedding day. I took a deep breath and sighed. "I have some paper cups," I said, closing the cabinet door.

She smiled. "Then paper cups it is…"

We began to eat. She was telling me about her life. She's a college student and a single mother. Her husband and father of her child had been murdered. Now, she was forced to raise her son alone. She works part-time, so that she can spend as much time as she can with her son.

The entire time that she was talking, I couldn't help but think about my day and all of the things that had transpired. Then, I looked at the woman sitting across from me. She was picking food from her teeth when she looked up and caught me staring at her. She smiled.

In that moment, I couldn't help but think about my wife and son, but then I looked at her again – a complete stranger who out of nowhere wanted to make sure that I never go "thirsty."

Playing with her paper cup, she said, "Tell me something about you."

"There's nothing to tell you," I said.

"Awwwwww, come on...I told you about me...tell me something about you."

"Look, Candy...I appreciate you being here, but I'm not the 'sharing type'."

She got on her hands and knees and crawled over to me. "If you're not the 'sharing type' then what 'type' are you?" She began to kiss me on the cheek, then her lips moved to my neck where she proceeded to kiss and lick me. I closed my eyes and allowed myself to enjoy the warmth of each touch. Feeling overwhelmed, I pushed her away from me. "Stop...I can't..."

She looked me deep into my eyes and said, "Don't worry. I promise. I'll be gentle."

When I fell asleep, I found myself dreaming about the young man, lying on the ground, reaching out to me – dying. The blood-soaked shirt that was clinging to the hole in his chest and then there was the man who did it to him. *"Why? Why did he shoot me?"* he cried out to me. *"Why?"* Suddenly, I awakened to find her lying next to me. As I tried to get up, I felt a burning sensation on the side of my neck. I touched it and felt teeth marks on both sides. *She wasn't gentle.* I thought to myself. I smiled.

She mumbled. "What…what's going on?"

"Shhhhhhh," I whispered. "Go back to sleep. I'll be right back." I got dressed, grabbed my gun, and drove over to the location where the boy's body was found. In the darkness, I stared at the ground – the concrete was still soaked in his blood. Suddenly, a voice came up from behind me. I pointed my gun at the figure walking towards me.

"Whoa, whoa, Officer…it's just me. The Neighborhood Watch Guy."

I took a deep breath and then returned my gun to my holster. "Why are you out here sneaking up on people? You could have got shot."

"Well, I'm glad that you didn't…could have ended-up like that guy," he said, pointing at the chalk-line on the ground.

I looked at him and frowned. "Why are you out here?" I asked.

"Just like you…I'm trying to keep the neighborhood safe," he said, pulling at the lapels on his shirt.

"Is that so?" I asked.

"Yep…THESE people are out of control…like a bunch of fucking animals…they need to be kept in check," he said.

I looked at him. "THESE people?"

"Oh, I'm sorry, but you know what I mean," he said.

Frowning, I said, "No, please explain it to me."

He looked around and said, "From one brother to another, I would think that you'd understand."

"Brother?" I asked.

"You know...brothers..." he looked around and then continued, "Yeah, these fucking animals need to be neutered...fucking breeding and sucking up all of the resources from us law-abiding citizens...it's a big job, but somebody has to do it," he said, proudly.

I smiled and asked. "So that person is you?"

"You...me...and all of the brothers in Blue," he confirmed.

"So you're a cop too?" I asked, being facetious.

"No, but I enforce the laws around here…these motherfuckers respect me and if they don't, they'll respect this." He raised up his shirt exposing the handle of a gun.

"Do you have a permit for that?" I asked.

"Yes, indeedy-do…I follow the law…not like these monsters," he said.

Sucking my teeth, I said, "Is that so?"

He smiled, flashing his coffee-stained teeth. "Yes, it is."

I was growing impatient, but I smiled, again. "So what really happened to this young man?"

"Oh, that little piece of shit?" he leaned in to whisper in my ear. "I asked him where he was going and he told me that he was going home, but he didn't look right to me…he looked suspicious…like the rest of them…so I told him to show me where he lived and he pointed, but I've never seen him around here before, so I told him to prove it…show me some ID and when he reached in his pocket, I shot him."

"That's it?" I asked.

Pulling his pants up on his stomach, he said, "Shit, that's enough. You see how quick they are at shooting each other. What he think about killing me ain't shit."

"But he didn't have a weapon," I said.

"Look...a weapon...no weapon...it's all a technicality...I did this world a favor...there's too many of those motherfuckers anyway...what's another dead one...his death wouldn't even have made it in the newspaper if I hadn't shot him. If one of THEM had of done it, he would have been a "blurp" on some website or a line in some newspaper."

I looked at him, growing incensed by the moment. "You know that was somebody's child?"

"They're all somebody's child...who cares? The world is a safer place without him."

I smiled. "Wow...that's ummmmmm...that's ummmmmm..."

He interrupted, "Amazing, fantastic, wonderful?"

"No," I said, grabbing him by the collar. "That's fucked-up."

He tried pulling away. "Wait…what are you doing?"

"You killed that boy for nothing," I said.

"No, I told you why I killed him. You should understand…," he said, still trying to get away from me.

I pulled him close to me. "Oh, but I do understand…" I paused and then continued, "I understand that you're a fucking asshole that need to be dealt with."

"Huh? What are you talking about?" he asked, looking around.

"You ever heard of an 'eye for an eye?'" I asked.

Confused, he asked. "You want my eyes? Why the hell do you want my eyes?" he asked.

"An eye for an eye, asshole…It's in the Bible. You never read the scripture about motherfuckers like you and how you should be dealt with?"

"No…no…I haven't read that one," he said.

"Well, in a nut shell…you took a life…now, the universe wants yours."

"Huh? What are you talking about? What universe?" he asked, looking around.

"It'll be a lot easier to show you. Now, shut up you piece of shit and get on your knees," I instructed.

"My knees? What are you talking about?" he asked, as beads of sweat formed on his forehead. "You want me to suck your dick? I'll suck your dick. Just pull it out…"

I shook my head. "As appetizing as that sounds, I'm going to pass. Now, again, get on your knees," I said, becoming impatient.

Finally, he kneeled down and got on his knees.

"I want you to look at that chalk-line. Someone's child was killed…murdered by your hands…and now, you are going to do the same thing to yourself."

His eyes widened. "What are you talking about?"

"You are going to kill yourself," I confirmed.

"Why would I want to do something like that?" he asked, confused and afraid.

"For the same reason you decided to kill him…to make this world a better place," I said, pushing him to the ground.

"But I can't kill myself…that's suicide…I can't get into Heaven if I kill myself," he said, seriously.

I began to laugh so hard that tears formed in my eyes. "Who told you that your motherfucking ass was going to Heaven? Your ass ain't going to Heaven…God don't want you and the Devil can't stand your punk-ass…," I said, still laughing.

He frowned and asked. "How do you know?"

I smiled. "Look around you. God is a figment of your imagination and Mr. Neighborhood Watch Guy...I...I am the Devil." I began to push him closer to the ground.

"Wait...what are you doing? Stop...you can't do this," he pleaded.

"Stop fucking moving," I said, as I positioned him within the chalk-line. I stood back and looked at him. "Perfect. Now, don't move." Then, with the sleeve of my shirt, I removed his gun from his waist-band and removed all of the bullets, but one. Then, I removed my gun. "Here put this in your mouth."

"I'm not going to do this...you can't make me do it," he said, with tears rolling down his face.

I leaned in. "You don't want me to do this...believe me...if I do it, I'm going to put a bullet in your ass for every year that that child was on this planet and that's going to be slow and very painful, but if you do it, it'll be quick."

"I don't want to die," he pled. "I don't want to die."

"And I'm sure that when that boy woke-up that morning, he didn't want to die either. Now, hurry up. My shift starts in a couple of hours," I said, looking at my watch.

"You can't be serious. You really want me to kill myself?" he asked.

"More now than I did a few minutes ago," I said, sighing.

I placed the gun in his hand, placed the barrel against his temple, and then placed his finger on the trigger. "Now, come on…you can do it. Just imagine yourself killing one of THEM."

He opened his mouth to say something, but before he could, the gun went off. I looked at him. He had a confused look on his face. *I bet he had questions too. A shame. I guess he'll never know.* I thought to myself.

The next day, they found him with his head splattered all over the concrete. When I arrived at the scene, they were still taping off the area.

I walked up and asked, "What happened?"

The officer responded, "Looks like a suicide."

"Isn't that the same guy who killed that boy the other day?" I asked, curiously.

"Yeah...I guess taking that boy's life took a toll on him...I can only imagine what he must have felt after killing that boy," he said.

If only you could imagine. I thought to myself.

"Well, there's no crime here. We should be wrapping this one up soon," the officer said.

I smiled. "Yep...no crime at all.

Chapter 13~

It was hot as hell. I tossed and turned all night. With sweat pouring off of me, I got up to get a glass of water. After filling the glass, I walked over to the window and looked outside. *Quiet.* There's no one outside. Everyone was locked "safely" behind closed doors.

I walked over and sat on the couch. In the darkness, I thought about my life. I thought about my job and all of the changes I've been seeing in my community. Things were bad and getting worse every day. It was getting to a point where no one was safe – not even a cop.

I got up to walk back to my bedroom when I looked down the hall at my spare bedroom. I stood there thinking about the young visitor. I smiled, because he was actually a funny guy. If he'd applied himself, he could have been a great asset to society, but instead he was an asshole now resting on the bottom of my barbeque grill. At least it'll be quiet, for now on.

I knew that I wasn't going back to sleep so, I slipped into some 'street' clothes, grabbed a bag of dirty clothes, and left into the night. I jumped into my car and then turned on the scanner. There were calls for assaults, battery, and rapes. Carefully, I listened to them. There were so many crimes being committed. The calls were ringing in my head like voices speaking out to me. I could see the victim's faces crying out to me, begging me to help them – to save them. I was tired, so tired of the crime – of the pain. Our communities being destroyed. No matter what I did, it would never stop. It would never stop.

I was at the laundromat doing some laundry when on the TV a story flashed across the screen....*Officer who is currently under investigation for shooting an unarmed teenager 10 times will not face charges in the recent shooting of another*...I looked up to find the cop who killed that boy the other night.

He was smiling and shaking the hand of some 'suit'. My blood began to boil. I didn't even finish folding my laundry. I just balled them up and threw them in a plastic bag.

I drove around for hours, hoping that the night air would calm my soul, but I was frustrated. The breeze was cool but not effective in soothing the storm that was raging inside of me. I knew what needed to be done.

That night, I stopped by the station and waited for him to come out. It was three hours before I saw him leave the building. When he walked out, he was laughing and talking with another officer. He didn't look like he had a care in the world. I watched him get into his car and then pull off. We drove for about thirty minutes before he stopped at a club on the far south-side of Chicago. He got out of his car. I waited a minute before following him inside.

He ordered a couple of drinks and was enjoying the company of a beautiful black young lady who looked to be in her early twenties. She was sitting on his lap and laughing as he rubbed her thighs. She hugged him and giggled as he rewarded her for her time by placing singles into her bra.

Quietly, I watched this exchange until the young lady stood and walked away. I wanted to talk to him, so I walked over. He looked up and said, "Heyyyyyy...look who's here."

I smiled and said, "Yeah...look who's here."

"If it ain't, Officer Friendly." He patted the seat next to him. "Have a seat...," he said, slurring his words.

A girl was walking pass. He slapped her on the butt and said, "Get me and my friend a couple of drinks...will you, doll?"

She faked a smile and said, "Sure, I'll be right back."

He looked at her and said, "They all love me...all of them."

I said, "Really?"

"Yep...'they' all love me and for the right price, they'll love you too," he confirmed.

I didn't like the way that he put an emphasis on the word 'they', because I knew what he meant by it. Some of the 'good old boys' in blue loved to come to clubs in the hood where they could get a little 'strange' before going home to their perfect little wives and their perfect little kids to their perfect little homes in the suburbs.

The waitress walked back over to the table holding a tray with two drinks. He laughed and said, "So where is his?"

No one else laughed.

The young lady was about to walk away when he said, "You forgot your tip."

She stuck out the tray so that he could place the money on it. He refused to put the money on the tray. He waved it around and said, "Bring them over here, honey."

She looked down. You could tell by the look on her face that this wasn't the first time that he'd asked her to play this game with him. She sighed before leaning over. He stuck the bill into her cleavage, grabbed her by the breast and said, "Keep 'em coming."

She looked at me and then looked away. She walked away and moments later, she arrived with a bottle and two glasses. After drinking the first two drinks, he poured two more.

He held up his glass and said, "A toast."

I hesitated, but then decided to join him. He continued, "A toast to justice." He reached over to make contact with my glass when I lowered my hand. He laughed. "What's wrong, buddy?"

I didn't respond.

"You need to loosen up. You and I...we got cause to celebrate."

I frowned. "We do?"

"It's like the good old days...don't you love the good old days? Days when folks respected the law 'cause they knew what'll happen if they didn't...those black bastards with their gold teeth and gold chains...pants hanging all off of their black asses...can't even afford a fucking lawyer...tying up the justice system with their bullshit...using wholesome tax-payers money...no more of that shit...shame we can't use the ropes like we used to..." He took his gun out and sat it on the table. "Naw...this'll do just fine."

I sipped from my glass.

He laughed so hard that his belly jiggled. "And that's another thing...all of this PC crap...I remember when it was okay to call a spade a spade...now, I gotta say Afro-American."

I corrected him. "That's African-American."

"Afro, African, who gives a shit...their black asses all look the same stretched-out in a pine box..." He could tell that I was staring at him.

I began to chew on my bottom lip, so hard that I was starting to taste blood.

The more that he drank the louder he was and the more belligerent he became. He laughed and turned drink after drink into the air. I nursed the same glass as he drank himself into a stupor. As the night was drawing to a close, he became more comfortable, more relaxed, and began to babble about his life, his job and the events of the month.

"You were there," he said. "He tried to attack me."

"Who?" I asked.

"That boy who was reaching into his pocket...you saw him...he had a gun," he said, slurring his words.

I became confused. I thought that he was talking about what happened earlier this week but the longer he spoke, I realized that he was talking about something else.

"What do they expect us to do? Wait for them to shoot us? Those monkeys shit on everything that they touch. My people brought them over here to our country and how do they thank us? By living on welfare and taking all of the jobs from the white man..." He tried pouring himself another drink but the bottle was empty. He signaled for the girl to bring him another bottle. While we waited, he leaned in and said, "Killing those fucking roaches is a public service...right bro?" He lifted his hand to give me a 'high-five' and almost fell out of his chair. He laughed. The girl arrived at the table. She put the bottle down and tried to walk away when he said, "Bitch, get over here."

She stopped, took a deep breath, and then turned around to face us. He took a twenty out of his wallet and said, "Get over here." She closed her eyes as if she was looking for something – the strength to walk away or just simply her pride but whatever it was, she couldn't find it because she walked back over and leaned in.

This time, he put the twenty into her cleavage and then pulled on her top until her breasts were exposed. She smacked his hand and then walked away. Shortly after, a big man walked up to the table. "You have to go, Jimmy," he said.

"Come on, Kong…just a little bit longer," he slurred.

Clearly, the bouncer didn't appreciate the nickname. He pulled Jimmy by the arm and said, "Get the fuck up and get the hell out of here." Jimmy flashed his badge and gun. "You know who the fuck I am…now, get your motherfucking hands off of me," he said snatching his arm away from the bouncer. The bouncer looked at me and said, "You better get your boy out of here."

I looked at Jimmy and said, "Come on…let's go." I pulled him to his feet and carried him out of the place. Once outside, I said, "You don't look like you should be driving…let me give you a ride."

He looked at me. Something in his face didn't look right. His eyes widened when suddenly he buckled over and threw up all over himself.

I jumped back to avoid the 'spray.' He threw up until he began to heave-up nothing but air. He looked pitiful. He began to cry. I lifted him and said, "Let's go."

When he got into the car, he immediately fell asleep. I looked into his wallet and found his address. I drove him to the address, parked in front of his house, and then tried waking him.

"Huh…what….what's going on?" he asked, incoherently.

I leaned over and pulled the door handle. The door swung open. "Get out," I said.

"Huh…oh hey, bro…where are we?" He looked outside and saw that he was safe at home. "Thanks, bro…thanks for the ride."

I looked at him. "Get out," I said, again.

"Huh? Ummmm okay…" He threw one leg out of the car.

I pushed him out. "Get out!" He stumbled and fell on the grass. Before he could say anything else, I leaned over and pulled the door closed. He was saying something but I didn't hear it. I pulled off.

In the rear-view mirror, I could see that he was still sitting on the ground. When I approached the stop sign, I thought back to that crime scene, remembered the body lying on the ground, and the mother's cries. I sighed, took a deep breath, threw the car in reverse, and went back. I jumped out and started to lift his body back into the car.

"Hey, you're back," he said.

I looked around and said, "Yeah…I'm back."

"Where are we going?" he asked.

"We're going to a party," I said.

He tried to buckle himself in, but couldn't. I looked at him and said, "You won't be needing that."

He laughed and said, "But it's the law…" He laughed so hard that he started to choke. I pulled off. He settled in and fell back to sleep.

Half-way to our destination, he began to mumble something. "Those niggers need to learn," he said.

I frowned, trying to keep my eyes on the road.

Groggily, he awakened and looked at me. "Yep, when those motherfuckers were in chains, they understood their place. Now, they got rights…what they got is the right to kiss my ass," he said, laughing.

My hands tightened around the steering wheel. I began to grit my teeth.

He continued. "I have to admit…I do love those big asses and lips…makes my 'shit' hard just thinking about 'em." He grabbed his crotch.

I began to roll my head because I began to feel a knot growing between my neck and shoulder blades. I drove around for an hour before we landed right where it all began. We parked. I looked around. It was quiet.

He sat up and then looked around. "Hey man…where we at?"

I smiled and looked at him. "We are home."

"Home? I don't live around these low-lifes," he said.

"Low-lifes…that's funny shit." I shook my head in disgust.

He laughed. "Man, wouldn't it be nice to grab one of those little ones and then string him up?" he asked. "Like the good old days?"

I smiled and said, "You know what? Let's do that."

His eyes widened. "Do what?"

I smiled again, "Let's string one up."

He began to salivate. "Man, don't play with my emotions."

I looked at him and said, "Your emotions are the last thing that I'm thinking about right now." I opened the car door and said, "I'm going to go over here real quick and when I get back, we can string one up."

He rubbed his hands and then licked his lips. "Okay...okay...don't keep me waiting."

I smiled. "Oh...I won't." I ran across the street and grabbed a jump rope that was sitting on the ground. When I came back, I began to blow my car horn.

He looked confused. "Why you doing that?"

"You want you a young one, right?" I asked. "You don't want to go and snatch one out of his bed. Naw, you want him to come to you, right?"

"Yeah…yeah…a young one...lynch him before he grows up."

I nodded. "Yeah, before he grows up."

He threw the car door open. I handed him the rope, watched him make a noose out of it, and wrap it around one of the big branches on the tree.

I blew the horn, again. Lights started to come on in some of the houses. He looked around. He was so excited. I activated the car alarm. Then, I turned on the radio and turned it up really loud. The 'bass' made the car shake. More lights started to come on in the houses. Nervously, he looked around. Doors, to the houses, began to open. A crowd started to form. I blew the horn again and more people came out.

Slurring his words, he said, "Which one of you niggers wanna volunteer?"

Confused, the people in the crowd looked at each other. One person asked, "What the fuck did he say?"

He looked at them and swung the rope. "I SAID which one of y'all wanna be a volunteer?"

They all looked confused and were becoming agitated.

Holding on to the tree, he continued, pointing into the crowd. "You...you...what about you?"

A young man touched his chest and asked, "Me?"

He smiled. "Yeah, you darkie...how about you?"

The crowd looked at him and then looked at me. I didn't say anything.

He reached into his pocket, pulled out a bottle and sipped before saying, "Come on, now...I need a nigger? Now, I need one of y'all to come and slide your neck in this hole..."

The crowd looked at me, again. I smiled, nodded my head, and then turned to walk away. The crowd parted like the Red Sea. They all stared at me as I walked through. Then, they turned their attention back to him.

Panicking and still holding the rope, he said, "Hey, where the fuck are you going?!!! We're brothers. We are in this together."

I stopped and looked at him before saying, "Yes, we are both cops and yes, we are both white, but no…you and I are not brothers." I turned and continued across the street.

The crowd surrounded him. They grabbed him and he began to scream. "You niggers better get your filthy hands off of me!!!!" He tried getting away from the crowd. "I'm a cop!!!! Damnit, do you hear me?!!! I'm A COP!!!!!" He looked in my direction and called-out. "Officer Friendly??? OFFICER FRIENDLY!!!!!!"

I watched as they wrapped the rope around his neck. Then, a few of them stood on the other side of the tree and pulled the rope until he was dangling in the air. His feet swung back and forth as he tried to free himself. He pulled at the noose until his face turned red. Everyone stood quiet as he struggled. People in the crowd began to pull out their cell-phones to take pictures and videotape the incident. His eyes began to bulge as his tongue hung out of his mouth. When his body twitched for the last time, I turned and walked away.

The next morning, I could barely open my eyes. I was so tired. I sat up, stretched, and scratched my ass as I strolled down the hallway. I poured the day-old coffee into a cup and then threw it into the microwave. When it was done, I grabbed the cup, the remote, and then turn on the TV. I walked over to the window and then threw the curtains open. I peered out into the street. I saw him – swinging back and forth with the word "Racist" written across his forehead. I took a sip from the coffee cup. I stared at him for a while and then said to myself, "I guess somebody should call the police," before I walked over to the couch to watch the morning news.

Chapter 14~

When I walked into my bedroom, for the first time, I thought about "closure." I thought about how it was time to say "goodbye" to her – to finally let them go. As I looked in the closet, I saw her clothing still hanging next to mine. As I pulled them out and then placed them on the bed, I noticed her uniform sitting in the back of the closet. I pulled the hanger towards me. I stared at her badge. I placed the jacket against my nose and inhaled, deeply. It still had traces of her perfume on it. I looked at it and then placed it back into the closet.

I began to fold the rest of her clothing when I noticed the dent in the mattress on her side of the bed. I tossed the clothes onto the floor and then climbed in on her side of the bed. The mattress wrapped itself around me and it felt like I was locked in her embrace. I closed my eyes and sighed. *I miss you so much.* Suddenly, my thoughts were interrupted when there was a knock on the door. I ignored it and nuzzled my face into the pillow. Then, there was another knock on the door. I crawled out of the bed, grabbed my gun, and then placed it under my shirt and under my belt. I was walking down the hall when out of the corner of my eye, I saw the baby's nursery. I closed my eyes and took another deep breath before proceeding down the hall. When I arrived at the door, I looked out of the curtain to find Candy standing on the porch. I opened the door.

"Hello, Cain…" she purred.

I smiled and said, "Hey."

She smiled. "Did I catch you at the wrong time?"

"Naw, everything is good," I said, moving to the side so that she could walk pass me. At the door, she proceeded to remove her blouse. She placed it on the couch. She removed her shoes and sat them next to the couch. She began to walk down the hall. She stopped and removed her pants and kicked them to the side of the hall. She removed her bra and then tossed it over her head – hitting me in the face. Then, she removed her panties. She turned, walked up to me, and placed them in my hands. I looked at them and then back at her beautiful bronze skin as she proceeded toward the bedroom. When she entered the room, she saw my wife's clothing on the floor. She paused and looked at me. "Is this okay?" she asked.

I paused for a second and then said, "Yes, it's okay. Let me take care of that."

I watched her as she stood in the bedroom window looking out into the moonlight – the beam of its light bouncing off of her eyes. The shadow of her body created a shadow on the bedroom wall. I could see her – all of her. She stood quietly, preoccupied, while studying the stars. I undressed, slowly, and then climbed into the bed - resting peacefully, attentively, watching her every move.

She was beautiful. There was sweat glistening on her face and watching it drip down into the curves of her body made me want her. I wanted to lick her. I wanted to taste every inch of her. She knew what she was doing to me standing there – teasing me. I wanted her so bad. She was all mine; at least for tonight.

I walked over to where she was standing and lifted her into my arms; cradling her legs around my back. I walked her over to the wall where I "entered" her. She moaned. She met my rhythm and when her legs tightened around my back, I walked her over to the bed where we both climaxed. When we were done, she walked over to the chair where she sat to watch me touch myself – now, teasing her. I watched her hungrily, wanting her again.

She ran her hand over the space between her thighs, smiling and amused as she playfully stroked herself. She knew that I was watching so she looked over at me and then licked her lips. I smiled. She wanted to play some more and I liked that, a lot. I moved to the end of the bed. She walked over to join me. I looked at her – touched her. I ran my fingers over the curves of her body as if I was looking for something. I placed my hand over her chest to find it – her heartbeat. Its song played loudly for me. It felt like it was beating just for me. I looked up at her face. I ran my hand over the warm spot between her legs. She took a deep breath and then exhaled. Her body went limp. I caught her and then carried her over to the bed. This amused and aroused me. I climbed in next to her and rested my head on her breast.

I thought about our first love-making session – wild and erratic, painful, but satisfying. While we rested, I thought about her. I thought about her family and I wondered if there was someone waiting for her - longing for her as I longed for her now. I wondered if they would miss her.

As my heart rate began to slow down and my pulse began to stabilize, I remembered each touch, each embrace, and each stroke. She was talking and I was listening – listening to her every word. She told me how she arrived at this place; roaming the earth for months, driven by her desire for peace and never finding it until now. As I rested, she shared with me the journey that led her to my arms. She spoke of the many nights that she wept as she dreamed of me, as she dreamed of giving me what I deserved.

Turning over to face me, she took my hand into hers, and gently kissed each finger. Whispering into my ear she said, "Do you know that I prayed for you? Prayed for this moment?"

Basking in my afterglow, I mumbled, "I bet you did."

Taking one of my fingers into her mouth, and sucking gently, she said, "Yes, I have waited a long time for you and here you are lying next to me."

I smiled and continued to listen. She went on like this for several minutes when my stomach began to growl. Tickled by this, she began to laugh. "Are you hungry, sweetie? Would you like for me to go get you something to eat before we start again?"

Looking her up and down, I said, "I already have everything that I need." Pulling her back onto the bed, I began to kiss her.

Moaning, she said, "That's it, baby. Take what you want."

Moaning, I replied, "Can I have it? All of it?" Gently, I began to nibble at her. I ran my tongue down the middle of her chest, kissing and biting her.

"Yes, baby," she moaned. Her breaths became labored, her chest rose, and her back arched. Becoming excited, she reached for me. I climbed back inside of her. We became one and as her rhythm met mine. She held me so tight, as if her life or my life, depended on it. I was becoming light-headed as if the blood was leaving my body.

She dug her nails into my back. I screamed. She screamed. I screamed. Then, she screamed, again. I could feel the blood pouring from my back. She kissed me, then she bit me, digging her teeth into my shoulder blades. I screamed and begged her for more. "Bite me harder," I begged.

"Yes," she agreed.

"Harder," I begged.

"Okay," she said.

"HARDER!!!!" I screamed.

She bit me so hard she almost drew blood. The pain felt so good, and while I enjoyed the pain the moment was suddenly interrupted.

She pushed me off of her, stood, and then said, "I'll be back."

I reached for her. "No, wait…I'm not done."

She kissed me and said, "I'll be back…I promise."

I smiled, trying to catch my breath. "Don't be long."

I threw my head back and then closed my eyes. Minutes later, I started to drift off when I heard it. When I looked up, she was standing over me – whistling.

I jumped up, searching for my gun.

"Looking for this?" she asked, pointing my gun at me.

"What are you doing?" I asked.

"I'm getting what's mine," she said.

"Yours? What are you talking about?"

She smiled. "I know what you did?"

Sitting up and looking at her, I said, "And exactly what it is that you think you know?"

She smiled and sat down next to me – still pointing the gun at me. "When they found him…with all of those bullet holes in his body…" she paused took a deep breath and then continued, "Did you know that when you handcuff someone, it leaves a mark?"

Now, I was smiling. "Yes, I do."

She stopped smiling. "They knew that a cop killed him…but you motherfuckers stick together…and since he had a record…since he killed your wife…they didn't bother to investigate…but I knew that it was you. I saw you at the crime scene…"

Frowning, I said, "So you befriended me…just to get close to me…so that you could get revenge for that low-life motherfucker? A motherfucker who killed my wife and son?"

She looked at me and said, "But that low-life motherfucker was MY low-life motherfucker and just like he didn't have the right to kill your wife and son…you didn't have the right to kill him."

Shocked, I said, "He was a fucking rapist. Clearly, he didn't give a shit about you…his ass was running the streets taking pussy from strangers. He would rather take the shit from somebody than to fuck you."

She became angry and hit me in the mouth with the butt of the gun. "Shut up…you don't understand. He's sick…he needs help."

Grabbing my mouth, I said, "He WAS sick…NOW, he don't need shit."

Grimacing, she placed the barrel of the gun to my forehead.

I looked at her trembling hands and said, "So you fucked me so that you can kill me?"

She shook her head. "No…I fucked you because I needed to be fucked. Killing you? Well, that's justice. You killed my man and now, I have to kill you."

I began to laugh.

She frowned. "What the hell is so funny?"

I shook my head. "Did you forget that I'm a cop? First, I'm always curious when folks show-up in the middle of the night in a Black teddy…" I laughed and then continued. "Unless, you're a 'working' girl or extremely damaged, desperate or crazy…nobody does that shit. Then, when you said that your man was murdered? I had to check you out. I found out that you are his baby's mama…I didn't want to put you on blast…watching you was entertaining…and watching you make a fool out of yourself while getting fucked was MY justice ."

Pissed, she pulled the trigger, but nothing happened. She began to fumble with the gun.

I shook my head. "Safety first…" I said, snatching the gun from her hands.

She threw her hands in the air. "You don't have to do this."

I flipped the safety switch. "Oh, but I must. What? You want to go back to fucking like this shit didn't just happen?"

"Can we?" she asked, whimpering.

I licked the blood from the side of my mouth and said, "You're crazier than that rapist-murderer that I put all of those holes in." I said, now, pointing the gun at her.

With tears in her eyes, she said, "But I'm sorry."

Pulling the trigger, I said, "Me too."

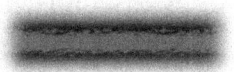

The next morning, I found myself covered in her blood as she rested lifeless at my feet. I leaned over her. Looking into her remaining eye, I could see the remnants of tears. With sympathy, I wiped the blood from her face.

"You're so beautiful. Do you know that?" I asked, but she didn't answer. Taking her arm and wrapping it around me, I fell asleep lying next to her.

When nightfall came, the moon awakened me. Crawling away from her side, I walked over to the window. As I stood there, I began to breathe heavily. I looked up at the sky and said, "No one will ever take your place." I looked over to where Candy lay waiting. I walked back over to her. Kneeling, I whispered into her ear. "I'll be back. Duty calls…"

Notes from the Author

First, by NO MEANS AM I ADVOCATING VIOLENCE, but as I wrote this, I couldn't help but wonder what it would be like if those who "kill, steal (take lives), and destroy," could see the pain that they cause through the "eyes" of their victims. This book explores the ugly side of human nature. It shows us how quickly that the "line" between good and evil can be crossed by anyone.

While the characters in this novel are fiction, we run across these people every day. The rapist, murderer, abuser, manipulator, a father pushed to his limits, an overzealous Neighborhood Watch Guy, and a cop – a human being – who under extreme circumstances ignored his vow and obligation to protect the public in turn becoming the man that we all fear.

Every day, each and every one of us get up, whether we are putting on the uniform or not, and we leave our homes with every intention of returning home safely, but unfortunately there are people out there waiting, police officer or civilian, to do us harm. We rely on the police to protect us, but because of everything that has happened, we've become a society of fear and mistrust.

As a mother, daughter, aunt, and mother-in-law of people who have served in the "war"...who has lost family members to "wars"...whether at home or abroad...I've seen what effects this can have on the person who picks up their guns everyday...say "goodbye" to the people that they love...to protect their country and their fellow citizens. The fear and horror that they must see and are exposed to, every day, can take a toll on anyone...on any human being. We must acknowledge that before they put on any uniform...they are human first. They are someone's father, husband, son, daughter, wife, mother, etc. They only have a second to make a decision that may cost them their life or the life of the person that they are charged to protect. The decision could be a matter of life or death.

When we see an unarmed citizen murdered for whatever reason, it frightens us...makes us angry...defensive...those among us that are good...after seeing this repeatedly cannot avoid being shaken...often times, becoming jaded against the victim or against those who victimize. It's a viscous cycle that sadly, we are all exposed to.

This in no way justifies the behaviors of those who suffer from "God complexes", or those who are afraid of the people that they've been hired to protect, or people who decide to take the law into their own hands or are afraid of the people that we're supposed to trust. But there are many who have been on the "front-lines" for far too long and need to acknowledge that – on both sides.

What people don't talk about is how death, be it unwarranted or justifiable, can have a big effect on everyone involved – this includes the officers, the families, the emergency personnel, doctors, etc. Death is never easy on anyone, but while it happens all of the time, we are asked to deal with it and move on, but we can't. Grief and fear has an interesting way of manifesting itself.

We must also be willing to acknowledge that when shit is wrong...shit is wrong. Cain is an example, like many throughout the novel and throughout the world, of when shit goes horribly wrong. While he may be a cop...a soldier fighting the wars in the streets...he is a man first and deals with loss like everyone else. The difference is, when your choices are limited, you deal with it the best way that you can. But what about those given a license to kill or when your options are far greater than the average human being? We might want to retaliate, but there are laws that keep us from taking the lives of other human beings whether they deserve it or not. Many may only find peace in an "eye for eye." It's hard, but at what point does it end? When there's no more "eyes" left?

The system is broken, but human beings created the system and they can fix it too. While "Black" lives are under siege, white and brown lives are too. Those in "blue" must remember that they've been hired to serve and protect and we must remember that before they put on their "blues", they are "black", brown and white too. They like to separate us by using terms like police and civilians, but in the end, while we may not all wear "blue"...being human unites us all.

Coming Soon...

Six Degrees of Separation
Spring 2017 in paperback
A preview of my next novel,

"Six Degrees of Separation (also referred to as the "Human Web") refers to the idea that, if a person is one step away from each person they know and two steps away from each person who is known by one of the people they know, then everyone is no more than six "steps" away from each person on Earth." -- Frigyes Karinthy

So now we must ask ourselves, "Where the hell did he come from?"

Prologue

Excuse me sir, do you have any change?" she asked, with the most beautiful blue eyes I've ever seen. I looked into my pocket and retrieved some small bills and handed them to her. It was cold out. Her teeth 'clicked' together as she thanked me. I had to admit that I felt sorry for her.

"Look, let me buy you a hot meal," I said.

"Oh, thank you, that would be nice," she responded.

We walked down to the corner diner. From the moment we entered, all eyes were on us. I ordered us some coffee to get us started. While we waited, the woman went on and on about the road that led her to this place — this moment in her life.

"He was a football player," she said, as if I gave a shit. "Yeah, he even went pro," she continued.

I looked around the room for the waitress who was taking so long to bring us our coffee that I was beginning to think that her ass took a trip to Columbia to hand pick the beans herself.

The woman sitting across from me was still rambling.

"I really loved his ass too…for real…no kidding. Everybody thought that I was only with him for his money, but I ain't no gold-digger.

No matter what they say," she spat through the gap in her front teeth.

The people in the diner watched and whispered as she took me down memory lane. She noticed it. I couldn't tell if she was embarrassed or not because her face was hidden under several layers of dirt. When the waitress finally arrived with the coffee, the woman excused herself, went to the bathroom, and when she returned it looked like she tried to clean herself up. She had pulled her matted hair back and she tried to wash her face. It was evident that she scrubbed really hard because now her pale skin was even redder than before. As I ordered, I could tell that the waitress was staring at me.

I didn't acknowledge her because I wasn't interested. When she realized that I wasn't going to give her the attention that she was seeking, she took the menus, placed them under her arm, rolled her eyes at the woman sitting across from me, huffed and then walked away.

Still talking, the woman said, "That motherfucker even had the nerve to be on the down-low. Man, I heard she cut the shit out of his ass."

Now, she had my attention. "She who?" I asked.

"The bitch he dumped to marry my fine ass." She smiled. "Then he dumped me to get back with her. That's why I'm glad that he's dead…with his triflin' ass," she said, like a person who was trying to make Ebonics a first language.

Curious, I asked, "So, she killed him?"

"Naw," she began. The waitress walked over with our plates. She paused and threw some fries into her mouth. "Like I was saying…naw, that motherfucker got him some 'jail-house justice.' They raped his ass to death. He was a loser in life. Now, he's a loser in

Hell." She went on like this for another hour.

I watched her thinking about what she may have looked like when she was younger. She was probably really pretty 'back-in-the-day.'

Now, she was just an empty shell — one of life's walking dead.

When she finished, I paid the tab and then we left the diner. I was about to walk away when she said, "I really appreciate what you did for me. Nobody has been that nice to me in a long time. Let me do something nice for you." She looked down at my crotch.

Frowning, I said, "There's nothing that you could do for me. Just take care of yourself."

"Please let me do something…it's the least I could do," she pleaded. She began to lick her lips seductively.

What a waste. I thought to myself. "Look, I'm good."

"Well, I promise that I'm going to do something really nice for myself. I might even use the money you gave me to go to the clinic and get myself cleaned up. Wouldn't that be nice? Change my life…become respectable," she said.

I looked at her. "Take care of yourself." I turned and walked away.

Later that evening, I was walking back in the direction where I left the woman. I walked passed an alley where I could hear someone both crying and laughing. I walked toward the sound. In the dark, it was hard to tell who it was. As I got closer, there she sat with a rope wrapped around her arm and a needle sticking out of her vein.

"Hey, I told you I was going to do something nice for myself," she said, recognizing me.

I looked at her; disappointed and angry. It was disgusting looking at her lying in the alley like trash that someone had thrown out. I leaned over her and then removed the needle from her arm. Lying on the ground next to her was a spoon, a lighter, and a couple of rocks that looked like heroine. I placed a 'rock' on the spoon and began to heat it. She laughed to herself. When the rock melted and became a liquid, I filled the syringe with it. As she mumbled and laughed to herself, I asked her for her name.

"My name is Sandy," she said, enjoying her

buzz. I hit the syringe with my finger, found her vein, and then plunged the needle deep inside of it. Initially, she smiled and closed her eyes. Suddenly, she looked at me as if becoming lucid just long enough to realize what was happening to her. I smiled at her. Before ramming the needle deeper into her arm, I said, "My name is Izrael. It was nice meeting you."

Acknowledgements

I am so lucky. What has started out as a simple dream has turned into something wonderful and it's all because of you.

A special "thank you" to all of the people who purchased my novels entitled *Never What it Seems, Autumn Leaves, Fallen Angel, Never What it Seems II – A Mother's Love, Kiss My Ass – This is Not Your Typical Self-Help Book, Peaches* and novel turned stage play, *Somebody Else's Baby*. I appreciate all of the wonderful reviews and feedback.

Much appreciation goes out to all of the libraries and Black-owned bookstores who have allowed me the opportunity to place my novels among all of the literary minds that came before me.

I am also grateful to all of the book-clubs. I have developed some wonderful relationships with readers here and abroad. Thanks for all of the encouragement, the pats on the back, and the jokes. You "guys" keep me laughing (you know who you are).

Hugs and kisses go out to my extended family — thank you (that includes the ladies who work at my bank, the nurses and the ladies who work at the front desk at my clinic, the ladies and men who work at my post office — grocery store, etc.).

To my family and friends (there are just too many to list) I haven't forgotten about any of you — thank you for always being there and for forgiving me when I couldn't call, visit, write, or email.

To all of you, thank you for believing in me and for your continued support. I'm extremely grateful to you for your guidance, patience, and understanding. I appreciate all of you.

-Diane Martin

Other Books

Other Titles

- *Never What it Seems*
- *Autumn Leaves*
- *Fallen Angel*
- *Never What it Seems II – A Mother's Love*
- *Kiss My A@@ - This is Not Your Typical Self-Help Book*
- *Somebody Else's Baby*
- *Peaches – Always Kiss Your Baby Goodnight*

Website:
http://dianemartin.weebly.com